A Smile for the Guil̄ and other stories

Khaled El Shalakany

Hello Everyone,

Most of these stories were previously published in other books of mine. I decided to gather them together and offer them in both Kindle and printed format at a very affordable price. What is new here is that as a recent convert to AI magic, I have used the Midjourney Bot (Discord) to generate the illustrations preceding each short story.

I fear that my stories, "Welcome to the Future" and 'The Last Message' may prove to be too prophetic. AI is coming, and (it/he/she/holiness) is simply brilliant. Maybe it is time for us *homo sapiens* to bow out of the scene before we destroy the planet. We could allow our electronic descendants to take over. It is possible that they will not exterminate us. I gather that with our petty squabbles, wars, and general idiocy, we could be quite entertaining to observe. I am not being pessimistic, simply realistic.

I want to write here a brief introduction to the two short stories at the end of this book. 'Thus Danced Zarathustra

– Part I and Part II'. These stories were entered as part of a competition with the theme being immigration. I decided to highlight the fact that *homo sapiens sapiens* , the human species that we are today, originated in Africa. So, all modern humans immigrated out of Africa, perhaps 50 or 40 thousand years ago, first to the Levant via Egypt and the Gulf of Oman, and then to Europe.

The title is of course inspired by Friedrich Nietzsche' book 'Thus Spoke Zarathustra', where a wise man decides to descend from the mountains to walks among people to speak the truth'. Many racists in the world are unable to appreciate or comprehend that we are all the descendants of a very small group of African immigrants.

Also inspired by Nietzsche's work, the composer Richard Strauss composed two pieces of music under the title 'Thus Spake Zarathustra'. The first movement 'Sunrise' was used by Stanley Kubrick in his famous sequence depicting the beginning of man's evolution with the use of the first primitive tool, a bone wielded by an ape as a weapon, in the film '2001 a Space Odyssey'. The second movement is called 'Song of the Night Wanderer'. I have based these two stories on these themes.

I hope you enjoy these flights of imagination, both mine and the Midjourney's Bot.

Khaled El Shalakany
Long Beach Resort, West of Alexandria
August 2023

Table of Contents

Exchange

Mahmoud had recently graduated from the Police Academy and was a lieutenant with the River Police. He was part of the frogmen squad, in other words the divers. He did not mind being the butt of jokes from his friends from the Academy who had been posted to the CID and other more prestigious departments. Mahmoud enjoyed his work. He liked the technical challenge inherent in diving in the murky waters of the Nile. Visibility was always poor, and the divers had to rely on a sixth sense of intuition to navigate down close to the muddy bottom of this mighty river.

The river itself seemed sometimes to Mahmoud to be a thing alive, reluctant to give up its secrets. No wonder the ancient Egyptians had an annual celebration for the Nile when offerings were made, some say even human sacrifices. He remembered once on a school trip to the Egyptian museum seeing a statue of the Goddess Anuket, the Goddess of the Nile. She was truly beautiful. She would receive the offerings made to the River. Some said that she took her lovers from among young men and women sacrificed in the annual River ceremony.

It was late afternoon one summer evening when the Giza River Police Department received an urgent signal that an accident had occurred at El Galaa Bridge. This was one of the bridges connecting Cairo and Giza, the two parts of the great metropolis. A trolley bus had fallen off the Bridge. This was a time of course in the late 1960s when the red and white electric trolley buses still roamed the streets of Cairo and Giza. When the electric pole on top of a bus got disconnected from the electric power grid, conductors would habitually jump out and reconnect the pole pulling on a rope attached to the pole. It appears that at a moment just like that, the driver got distracted and crashed into the narrow Bridge's short metal fence.

When Mahmoud and his squad reached the scene, they could see that the bus had fallen close to the west end of the Bridge, and slipped on the embankment right into the water. It was deep there and when the bus had finally stopped sliding and had settled onto the muddy bottom, the white top of the bus could not be seen from the banks of the river. In typical Egyptian fashion immediately after the accident a huge crowd had formed on the bridge and the banks of the river. There were quite several police officers present on the scene, and everyone seemed to be shouting and gesticulating at the same time.

The divers were ordered immediately into the water. But it was late, as is usual in Cairo's desert climate, darkness had fallen very quickly. Mahmoud knew right away that it was useless. Their job would not be to save lives, but to recover bodies. He connected the safety rope to his waist harness and slipped into the cold water. He was very tense as he went deeper and switched on his powerful underwater lantern. He could make out the bulk of the bus beneath him and he went down and into the bus through one of the windows.

As Mahmoud expected there were many bodies jammed inside the bus. He could imagine the panic and horror of these last moments as the bus slid into to the muddy waters of the river, the screaming and frantic attempts to get out and the pushing and shoving as people tried to get to the windows. He got hold of one of the bodies and pulled it out of the window. It was man in a full suit. Mahmoud tried not to look at the face. He got the body out and pulled himself back to the shore using the rope.

The gruesome task continued well into the night and Mahmoud made several more dives. On his sixth dive Mahmoud worked his way to the back of the bus. There in the path of the light of his powerful lantern he could make out a group of bodies at the very back. It was a horrible sight, a mother and her three children all huddled together. To the left of the doomed family there was a young woman. While all the bodies were contorted in the tortured shapes in which the drowned are commonly found, this young woman appeared to be sitting down.

Mahmoud shone his lantern onto the young woman's face, and he jumped back startled. She had a truly beautiful face, and her black hair floated above her head, but what startled Mahmoud were her eyes. They were wide open and appeared to be looking straight at him. Mahmoud had seen many dead faces, and the eyes even when opened had that vacant glassy look of the unseeing. But these lovely eyes were anything but dead. Mahmoud could have sworn that there was life behind these eyes. He was mesmerized. When the woman raised her right arm and beckoned him to her, Mahmoud screamed. He could hear the scream in the water around him.

Mahmoud's mind raced in a panic, was that a reflexive muscle movement, or was the young woman by some miracle still alive. He moved closer and closer, and when he was just in front of her, her right arm moved suddenly, it was too quick for him, and before he could react, she had held him by his left wrist. He tried to pull away, but it was impossible, it was as if he was chained to the woman. Looking at her, he could see that her face was vaguely familiar. Then he remembered she looked exactly like Anuket. She pointed to the drowned mother and children and then looked at him gesturing with her arm questioningly. Mahmoud understood immediately, and it did not take him too long to respond. He nodded and could see her smile a radiant smile and nod back at him.

The newspapers next day all had pictures of the tragic accident, but there were also pictures of the miracle, the rescue of a mother and her three children who apparently were trapped in a huge air bubble at the end of the bus. The papers also carried the story of the heroic death of lieutenant Mahmoud who was martyred during the rescue operation. Apparently after guiding the family one by one to the surface, his safety rope was cut, and he was dragged down by the current.

Mahmoud's body was never recovered.

Draft Report on Recent Problems at the Ministry of Crime

His Criminal Excellency

Minister of Crime

Dear Minister,

The whole world was amazed and awed when our great country was the first country to legalize criminal activity. The Ministry of Crime was set up to register criminals and put in place the new revolutionary cost/benefit approach to criminal activity. Registered criminals would submit their plans for forthcoming crimes. Each plan was analyzed for probability of successful implementation, and if the probability exceeds 60%, the Ministry would then either pay the planner the scheduled compensation rate in order not to commit the crime or give the green light to proceed in return for payment of 60% of the social cost of the crime. The compensation rate depended on the type of crime was usually set a percentage of the cost to society should the plan have been implemented. For petty crimes the percentage was quite low. For serious crimes and acts of terrorism the percentage could go up to 70% or more. Things went quite smoothly for the first few years. The Department of Bribes, for example, boasted at least ten thousand registered government employees in the first year alone. The Department had a very efficient system in place. The prospective bribe giver would apply to the Ministry to facilitate his business with the Government.

The total value of all bribes required would be calculated based on the sector of business, scale of the project and other relevant factors. Suitable bribe takers would be identified from the Ministry's roster of bribe takers. They would then be paid 50% of the total bribe amount. It was a clear win/win situation. The bribe giver was ensured success, and the Government realized some additional revenue.

Serious problems started to crop up. For example in the Murder Department it became quite difficult to calculate the social cost, police time in investigation, the loss to society resulting from the removal of the victim, prison costs in case of apprehension of the perpetrator etc. In some cases the social cost was negative, in other words society stood to gain from the murder of the intended victim. This was found to be the case in many instances where the intended victim was an employee of the Ministry of Crime itself or a criminal registered with the Ministry. It also became quite difficult to spot applicants who had no intention of killing their spouse or whoever they claimed was their intended victim, particularly if the applicant was not registered with the Department of Fraud. However, the most serious problem was the actual number of registered criminals, this escalated to about 82% of the adult population. It appears that people find it easier to live a life of crime than continue to be potential victims. The sheer cost of maintaining the system is now too high for Government resources. That is why I have been asked to prepare a report with my recommendations.

The above is a draft of the introduction to the Report that you have commissioned me to prepare. I have left my recommendation open. As you know I have been one of the first experts to register with the Department of Bribes, and accordingly please regard this letter as a formal application for a substantial bribe (I am sure that you appreciate that the social costs at risk are extremely high).

I await your bribe and instructions.

Yours sincerely,

Do not ask for whom the Loudspeakers Blare

Until perhaps the early eighties, Basoos was a quiet a village on the northern outskirts of Cairo. The relentless expansion of Cairo 'the Victorious' eventually enveloped Basoos, with many thousands moving in from Shubra and other neighbouring districts of the City. Countless small workshops sprung up in Basoos, which became also known as 'little Taiwan' for the variety of products (many of which are counterfeit) produced there. Still the peasant core of the original village survived, and one could still see *gamoosas* (water buffalos) crossing the high road along with a number of donkeys, carts and other village type modes of transportation.

Haj Said always prided himself on being an original *Basoosi.* That is not to say that he did not benefit from the transformation (he owned two apartment blocks and made a good living from selling automobile spare parts). *Haj* Said was known as a pious man, careful to perform all his daily prayers, attending Friday prayers without fail, fasting during Ramadan, and of course making the great pilgrimage to Mecca (hence the title of *Haj*). As are most Egyptians, he was very superstitious. blood- soaked hands with five fingers blocking the evil eye adorned his buildings, and he wore a *hijab* around his neck with verses from the Holy Koran to protect him.

In Basoos there are tens of small prayer rooms and two large mosques. They all have very powerful loudspeakers, used to broadcast the call to prayers five times a day. A prayer room and a loudspeaker present a relatively inexpensive way to reserve a 'palace' in heaven (the reward for those who set up God's houses on Earth). At dawn each day *Haj* Said would lie in his bed and listen to the loudspeakers calling the faithful out of their beds to pray, with the special call made only at dawn 'prayer is better than sleep'. At seventy years of age, *Haj* Said no longer went out to the mosque for the dawn prayer, he would lie in his bed and listen to the cacophony of sounds coming out of the loudspeakers. It was regrettable that some of the faithful who set up loudspeakers had truly ugly voices, totally unlike the original *muezzins* who were supposed to have beautiful and melodious voices.

One of the customs that survived from Basoos's village past was the announcement over the loudspeakers every morning after dawn prayers of the names of those who had died the day before or during the night so that people would go to the funerals and pay their respects. Everyday *Haj* Said would listen carefully and thank Allah that his name was not among those whose demise was heralded by the loudspeakers. One cold winter morning, he was listening as usual, when he heard '*Haj* Said father of Fikri has passed on to Allah's mercy – burial today after noon prayers... Eternity is for Allah only...'

At first, *Haj* Said thought he had not heard correctly, but when his name was repeated again, he sat up in bed in a cold sweat. His wife the *Haja* was sleeping next to him. He tried to wake her, but he could not touch her. His hands seemed to be made of something ethereal like smoke and passed through her body. He screamed and shouted at her, but she did not wake. *Allah preserve us, I am dead* he thought. *But where is Azraeel the reaper of souls, why is my soul still on this Earth?* The next few moments were filled with a terror like he has never experienced in all his years. Suddenly he heard the Loudspeakers call to dawn prayers...'prayer is better than sleep. Prayer is better than sleep'. *Praise be to Allah, it is not morning yet, I was dreaming ... it was all a dream...*

That same morning, after the dawn prayers, the people of Basoos all heard the loudspeakers blaring out *Haj* Said's name. The funeral took place after the noon prayers, and afterwards his wife the *Haja*, dressed in black, received friends and family who came to pay their respects. In tears she told of how when she woke up just before dawn, a blessed hour as the Loudspeakers were calling people to prayers, she found the *Haj* dead with a smile on his face, and then she would say with a sad smile:

"The *Haj* died peacefully in his sleep as befits a pious man".

The Bittersweet Dreams of Captain Nimitz

UN Office of the Secretary General   August7, 2026

Dr. M Morkowitz

Director

Lubjana Mental Institution

For the Criminally Insane

Dear Dr. Morkowitz,

We have recently received a handwritten note from one of the patients at your institution. The note may prove useful to doctors handling his case, and accordingly its contents are reproduced hereunder.

QUOTE

Dear Secretary General,

You probably have not heard of me. I am Balbo Majorink an astro-physicist formerly with the Physics Department at the University of Budapest. I have been an inmate of the Lubjana Mental Institution for the past two years. After great difficulties and at considerable risk to myself and others I have managed to smuggle this note out. It is of the utmost importance that you act immediately in this matter, nothing less than the dreams of mankind is as stake.

Before I was incarcerated in this horrible place, and over a period of many years I had conducted personal research with the aim of tapping into a vast reservoir of human energy that few are aware of. Sir, I have established through meticulous scientific methods, that dreams are composed of intricate electromagnetic fields released in the human brain, and that these fields remain in existence even after the dreamer awakens, and theoretically for all time, long after the dreamer has ceased to exist. These dream fields join countless other dreams in an incredible stream of energy that flows through the stratosphere. My aim was to tap into that stream, and after years of experimenting, I finally succeeded.

Sir, let me tell you that living other people's dreams can be an extremely traumatizing experience. I still wake up in a cold sweat from the mere memory of Alexander the Great's dreams. They were full of the screams of countless hapless women and children as they were hacked to death by his armies' cold swords of steel. I have lived the grandiose dreams of Napoleon, where Paris was the center of an empire that strung across the whole Earth. I have seen Hitler's confused dreams where a race of super humans enslaves all others. I have even enjoyed the grand feasts dreamt of by the poor and the hungry.

I decided not to publish my findings, after all can we really deprive human beings of their dreams, when they have already been stripped of almost everything else that is human. My problems started when I tapped into the dreams of Captain Nimitz, the Commander of the USS Swordfish, a nuclear submarine stationed in the Mediterranean. He had a recurrent dream, it always started with a beautiful image of a huge field full of red roses that covered the land as far as the eye can see, and then suddenly hundreds of mushroom-like clouds rise into the heavens, full of a light of such intensity, that even in the dream one cannot look at it directly. Before long I realized that Captain Nimitz was insane, he was obsessed with the idea of bringing an end to our world through a nuclear holocaust. When this dream started to occur at increasing frequency, intermingled with the launch sequence for his submarine's missiles, I knew that there was no time to lose, I had to act.

All my attempts to contact Captain Nimitz's superiors failed. I realized that the only solution was to try to stop him before it was too late. I assure you that when I shot and killed Captain Nimitz in Cyprus two years ago, I was solely motivated by the desire to save our race. I am not the raving lunatic the Court judged me to be. Now under electric shock treatment, I have started to talk, my secret is out. The doctors at Lubjana are gradually realizing that there may be some truth in my ravings about the great river of human dreams. I am certain that before long I will be forced to divulge all my findings. Imagine what power any government with this knowledge would have if it could tap into people's dreams. I was visited last week by an American scientist, who I suspect works for the CIA. I am told that he has asked for further visits to be arranged. Rest assured Sir that I will never surrender my secrets, I would rather die than betray our dreams. Sir, you must act now, immediately before it is too late. I am sure that under UN protection I could demonstrate to the whole world this scientific reality and ensure that our dreams remain protected.

Dr. Balbo Majorink

End Quote

Yours sincerely.

T. Longine

Secretary to the Secretary General

September 7th, 2005

Dear Mr. Longine

Thank you for your letter of August 13th, 2005. I regret to inform you that Dr. Majorink was found dead hanging in his cell two weeks ago. While it is true that Dr. Majorink was indeed visited by a scientist from a prominent University in the United States and that the visit was arranged through the US Embassy in Budapest, the visit had nothing to do with Dr. Majorink's delusions about dreams and was conducted solely for the purpose of psychiatric research. It is truly unfortunate that such a brilliant scientific career ended in severe mental illness and suicide. Solely for the purpose of completing our medical records, we would appreciate it if you would let us know immediately if Dr. Majorink had sent you any other information, for example, the location of his research documents.

Your cooperation in this matter would be highly appreciated.

Yours sincerely,

M Morkowitz MD

Director

Lubjana Mental Institution

For the Criminally Insane

The Comrade and the Blue Buddha

It was 3 am on a bitterly cold morning of January, 1968, and Comrade Ten Zin was not a happy man. In fact, he was miserable. Chairman Mao, the Great Helmsman had let loose the dragon. The Cultural Revolution was sweeping across China. Nothing was sacred to the students except the Chairman's Red Book. In Lhasa, the Potala Palace itself had been sacked a few weeks ago, and across Tibet tens of monasteries have been destroyed. Invaluable relics have been lost. The Comrade had always been a Party man, but this new wave of madness was too much. Has the Chairman finally 'lost it'. How can the Peoples Republic rise to glory, if all its heritage is being torn down.

As head of the Lhasa local Communist Party Committee, Ten Zin knew that later this morning the crazed students had organized a march to Chokpori, in the heart of Lhasa to demolish the Blue Buddha. Removing some of the relics from the monasteries, melting statues into gold and silver to feed the starving people was one thing, but defacing the Blue Buddha painted hundreds of years ago on the face of the Chokpori rock, was another thing.

The Blue Buddha was unique in all of Tibet, and a most revered and sacred site. His was the gift of counsel in need. The confused, the lost, all those seeking direction in life, would come to Chokpori and would prostrate themselves before the Blue Buddha, and He would unfailingly show them the way. Ten Zin knew full well that any damage to this site will lead to an uprising in Lhasa, and the loss of countless lives, not to mention a serious setback in the Party's efforts to win the peoples' 'hearts and minds.' What to do? He had been unable to sleep for days now. He knew that any direct opposition to the students would brand him as a revisionist, with exile to a hard labour camp or perhaps even execution.

Although a Tibetan, Ten Zen was never a religious man. Since he was eight years old, he had been raised and educated in Beijing (where he attended the Fine Arts Academy and some of his professors even thought of him as a painter with considerable talent for painting portraits). He only returned to Tibet after 1959 when China took over, and the 14th Dalai Lama (Ocean of Wisdom) escaped to India. But for some unknown reason, on this cold morning Ten Zen decided to visit the Blue Buddha's site. He had already ordered the whole area cordoned by the Police, and thus he stood quite alone before the Chokpori rock face and gazed awhile at the serene countenance of the Blue Buddha. Suddenly and impulsively, he looked around, made sure no one was in sight, and prostrated himself on the hard ground.

Involuntarily the mantras of his early childhood came to mind 'Um Ma Ni Pe Me Hum' he repeated over and over.

They say that human words cannot describe 'satori' that flash of enlightenment that surges through a person when for a brief moment, that person becomes one with the infinite Void. Perhaps that is what happened to Ten Zin that morning. Accounts are vague. What is known for certain is that next morning, the students marched up the Chokpori hill to the sacred rock intent on destroying the painted rock face. There they saw the Blue Buddha in all His splendour, but...but there was something terribly wrong, the face of the Blue Buddha looked strangely familiar. It was a tremendous shock; the face of the Blue Buddha was exactly the face of Chairman Mao.

It is said that many of the Tibetans among the students threw themselves to the ground and prayed. No one could dare touch the face of the Great Helmsman, and thus the Blue Buddha was saved. Some say that the Blue Buddha always looked like Chairman Mao, and that the Great Helmsman was in fact a reincarnation of the Buddha.

Others say that the face of the Blue Buddha miraculously changed on that fateful cold morning. No one knows for sure, except perhaps Ten Zin. It is said that Ten Zen resigned from the Communist Party shortly after these events and joined the Gelugpa monks (Yellow Hats Sect), and eventually became the abbot of the Drepung monastery and a most famous and respected Lama.

It is also said that he never lost his talent for painting portraits, and many of his paintings still adorn the walls of his beloved Drepung monastery.

The Red Pyramid

Hussien was desperate, he had only three hours of darkness remaining, and despite the frantic digging for hours now, he had not yet uncovered the slab leading to the sacred chamber.There he stood 170 hands from the center of the north face of the Red Pyramid, precisely as described in the *Sinti* scroll, and no slab! Few people are aware that the first perfect pyramid in history preceded the *Khufu* great pyramid of Giza. *Khufu*'s father the Pharaoh *Snefru* built the Red Pyramid around 2580 BC. After botching their first attempt at Dahshour, *Snifru*'s architects finally succeeded, they got their calculations right and produced the masterpiece that was the Red Pyramid.

No one knows the exact function of an ancient Egyptian pyramid. Theories and speculations are numerous. Were they monuments built by aliens, giants, or some other mysterious beings, or were they just grandiose tombs for the Pharaohs. A few, including Hussein, believed that they were magical instruments, harnessing the mystical forces inherent in the unique pyramid shape, and designed to transport the souls of men to Orion's constellation in the heavens, where they can reside in eternity with *Osiris* the God of the afterworld.

Hussein, a gynecologist by profession, and an avid amateur Egyptologist, has had only one driving passion in his life ever since he set eyes for the first time on the Red Pyramid. He immediately felt its power and was determined to uncover its secret. He was certain that the true function of the pyramids was embodied in this first masterpiece, the prototype of the hundreds that followed. Years of research led him, an amateur, to discover the message imbedded in *Sinti*'s funeral scroll, lying neglected in the basement of the Egyptian museum. Sinti was a low-ranking priest from *Snefru*'s time, and was never given serious attention by researchers.

It was nearly by accident that Hussien noticed the cryptic message imbedded in *Sinti*'s funeral scroll. Halfway down the scroll, there was a strange text that deviated from the standard text of the book of the dead. It read: '*Sinti* has been to the sacred chamber 170 hands from the north face of the Shinning Pyramid and will reside for eternity with *Osiris*'. There could be no doubt that *Sinti* was referring to the Red Pyramid's sacred chamber. It took months of preparation for Hussien to finally get his chance to try out *Sinti*'s directions, selecting a time of year when there were no expeditions working in the area, and bribing the sole policeman on night duty.

Hussein thought he had enough time working through the night. But it was already three o'clock in the morning and he was exhausted. Suddenly he stopped digging, he could feel something solid under his shovel. He carried on at a faster pace, and there finally in the moonlight he could make out the slab. Two hours later, Hussien stood at the opening of a narrow deep shaft that he had uncovered under the slab. He unrolled and fixed a rope ladder and with a powerful battery powered lantern started the long decent down. As he was going down, he sensed some movement on top, and could see the moonlight disappear as someone or something pushed the slab back into place, and trickles of sand fell around him.

Apparently, the hole he had dug was being filled again. For a moment he panicked, but he knew it was useless to try to ascend now. He was trapped, and the only way he could move was deeper down the shaft. Some 30 meters down, when he felt that the shaft would never end, his feet touched the floor of a chamber. As he turned the lamp around he could see drawings and hieroglyphs in fantastic colours. He rushed into an adjacent chamber, and he could see that it was the sacred chamber, the first ever to be discovered under any of Egypt's pyramids.

For a long time, he stood as if in a trance. There to the north of the chamber was the shaft, according to his theory leading directly to Orion's belt, and the magic words were all around him on the walls screaming to him in brilliant colours mixed by human hands many thousands of years ago. The shaft behind him had filled up with sand. There was no escape now. Hussein knew that there was only one way out of that underground chamber. He started reading slowly repeating the formula on the walls, over and over.

Some hours later at the end of his shift, the policeman on night duty at the Red Pyramid site, signed out and started the long way home. First the three kilometers walk to the *Sakara* road, and then a bus ride to Giza. Although his regulation boots were hurting his feet, he was not unhappy. With the money he got from the strange *effendi*, he was going to buy two kilos of meat, a surprise treat for the wife and the family. He never even wondered where the *effendi* went to, he assumed that he left during the night. From experience with previous nocturnal visitors, he guessed the *effendi* had a hot date and wanted some privacy or perhaps he wanted a quiet place to smoke some hash or bango.

Over the next few days some Cairo newspapers carried a small news item about the mysterious disappearance of one of Cairo's leading gynecologists. His car was found parked and empty on the main *Sakara* Road. Foul play was suspected. All the dailies, however, featured the astounding reports coming out of various observatories around the world about the sudden appearance of a new bright star in Orion's belt. Prominent scientists commented that this was the result of a black hole collapsing and giving birth to a new star, thousands of years ago (Orion's belt is approximately 2000 light years from Earth). The scientists explained that this was the reverse of the super nova process.

They even hinted that this phenomenon held the key to finally understanding the origins of the Universe and the beginning of time itself.

A Cat and a Dog

The Cat was called Spotty because she was a spotted little cat. K found her as a day-old kitten lying under his car. He could not leave her there, so he took her home. He and his wife fed her and nurtured her. Soon she was a sprightly and playful little kitten. Like all cats she quickly developed a few eccentric habits. At night she would jump on to his bed and start licking his hair. This did not make for a very restful sleep. When he would return home after a long day's work, she would without fail start to play by going through a series of mock attacks against him. He would also play along and step backwards and sideways.

There was, however, a very serious problem. K and his wife kept a very big dog in the garden. A German Shepard called Prince. The dog was truly a prince...simply beautiful. Prince was a great guard dog and had a fearsome reputation in the whole area. K and his wife lived in a villa overlooking the Nile, and Prince ever diligent would sometimes jump into the river and swim growling towards a fishing boat that would have dared come too close to the shore. The poor fishermen, scared out of their wits, would without fail quickly row away. Unfortunately, Prince did not tolerate any other animals in 'his' garden. Quite frequently Prince would attack and kill a dog that would have had the misfortune of venturing into the garden. Similarly, Prince would kill without mercy any cat that it found in the garden.

Despite this very aggressive and deadly nature, Prince was very gentle and friendly with K and his family as well as the gardener and his family. K loved his dog Prince and somehow tried to make the dog accept the presence within the house of Spotty the little kitten. He would place Spotty in a cat box, for her own safety, and take her out to the garden and try to introduce her to Prince. Somehow, he could feel the envy that Prince had for the kitten. Spotty after all lived inside the house and enjoyed the family's attention all the time, while Prince was restricted to the garden and got to be with the family only occasionally when they were leaving, arriving, or sitting by the Nile in the garden.

The kitten was somehow bedazzled by the huge dog. She was not afraid, only very curious. Quite often K would see Spotty sitting at one of the windows looking through the glass outside at the dog. Prince sometimes also would be looking back at the kitten. The fear for Spotty was a constant worry for K. He gave instructions to the cleaning lady who came twice a week to make sure that Spotty did not sneak out to the garden. He could feel that Spotty wanted very much to get to the garden. One day K came back from work and panicked because Spotty was not found in the house. Everybody started looking for Spotty, and he feared the worst. Finally, K found Spotty curled up in one of the drawers in a huge chest of drawers in his bedroom. He was greatly relieved.

K's attempts to make Prince accept Spotty failed. He did not have the courage to take Spotty out of her box in the garden, he was worried that Prince would pounce before he could react. Then there came the inevitable tragedy. He was traveling abroad when he got a call from his son A that Spotty had managed to sneak into the garden and was attacked by Prince. A took Spotty to the vet, but it was hopeless, she was put to sleep.

K was devastated. He could never have imagined that he would be so grief stricken by the death of a cat. He returned to his home and immediately felt that there was something important missing. The playful mock attacks the purring of Spotty as she curled on his or his wife's shoulders. It was a sad time for him. When he went out to the garden, he could not bear to look at Prince. Somehow, he had unrealistically imagined that Prince would not attack Spotty. Prince was a very intelligent dog, and he must have known how much K loved Spotty.

K could not help his negative feelings towards Prince. He could no longer bring himself to pat him on the back or rub behind his ears. It was strange, but Prince seemed to feel all that negativity. He took to sitting alone sulking and literally stealing furtive glances at K, who could have sworn they had a guilty look. Soon afterwards Prince became very ill. The vet could do nothing as a malignant growth was slowly robbing Prince of life. Prince died a few weeks later.

K buried Prince in the garden close to where he had buried Spotty, and oddly enough he had tears in his eyes.

Obelisks

The first one to light up was the one in Rome, the one that Julius Caesar had brought back as a gift from Cleopatra. It lay at the center of Piazza del Popolo, the most beautiful square in Rome, and perhaps in the whole world. It was early evening on what was a hot July day. The piazza was filled with people. Suddenly there was a low humming sound. As the sound grew louder some people started to get worried and started looking around for the source. A young child was first to notice the blue light surrounding the obelisk at the center of the square. At this point people realized that the sound was coming from the Obelisk itself. It was lit up all in a shimmering blue light, pointing straight up to the sky, it looked like a spaceship.

The people were quite amused and thought this was a new sound and light show organized by some Italian tourist board or authority. Eventually the police were called in and the square was cordoned off. Italian scientists were called to the scene. After two days of running various tests, they declared that they were unable to explain neither the source of the sound nor the light. During the following weeks scientists from other countries were invited to inspect the Obelisk that was still all lit in blue and emitting a humming sound. Again, there was no success.

A few weeks later the same thing happened with the Obelisk at the Place de Concorde in Paris. The phenomenon then occurred in London and then

Washington D.C. Within the course of seventeen weeks a total of twelve obelisks had lit up, three of which were in Egypt. A satellite picture revealed that there was a pattern in the location of the twelve obelisks. The twelve points represented the outline of the Orion Constellation, with Orion's belt coinciding with the location of the three great pyramids of Giza.

Now in the early 21st century, nearly 200 years after the industrial revolution and decades after the onset of the information and communications revolution, mankind was confronted with a phenomenon that was scientifically totally inexplicable. Scientists from all disciplines continued to run tests and work around the clock, but there was not even a hint of an explanation for what was happening to these huge basalt structures pointing to the heavens.

Some Christian priests declared that it was a miracle, a sign from God. An obscure religious cult in Arizona called the Children of Isis declared that it was a sign from the mother Goddess that she had returned to console a troubled humanity. Religious leaders were joined by astrologers and spiritual healers in presenting a variety of theories to interpret the blue light and the low humming sound. Endless discussions and debates ensued in the media. The fact that the pyramids of Giza were aligned with the three main stars of Orion's belt was pointed out again and again by Egyptologists. Still, no one could provide any explanation. Humanity was simply clueless.

The phenomenon continued for about three more months, and then just as it had started it ended. First the obelisk in Rome, then the others in the same sequence stopped emitting the sound and the light. Further endless spiritual and religious debates ensued. Some said it was the end of time, some said it was the beginning of a new era. Others declared that humanity in proving unable to decipher the message had failed a test and missed an opportunity to join a galactic community of sentient beings located around the Orion constellation.

Matters became more confused when immediately following the end of the sound and light emissions a super nova explosion was observed in the Orion constellation. As Orion lies about one hundred light years from Earth, the super nova had already occurred one hundred years earlier.

A professor of abstract mathematics who had been working on the audiovisual and other recordings of the obelisks' phenomenon finally managed to identify a time-space pattern in the sequence and location in which the obelisks were lit up which correlated to the frequency of the humming sound and the frequency of the blue light. When this pattern was mathematically deciphered with reference to ancient Egyptian language, a simple message was produced.

The message was 'goodbye sweet home'.

Ongandu's Appeal

What happened that night would haunt me for the rest of my days. Listen to me carefully, I was never a racist, nor do I believe, as some do, that a black man carries within the blackness of his skin some inherent inferiority. So of course, I did not accept the way Ongandu was treated that night when we were arrested in Bourbon Street.

I had finished my piece on the sax at the Old Cat, and having drunk a few too many got into one of my usual Saturday night fights. This time it happened to be Ongandu the new drummer of the band, fresh from Africa with his tom-tom drums. Before long Ongandu and I were locked up in the holding cell at the downtown police precinct. I do not know where Ongandu was from exactly, I recollect someone saying once that he was from Mozambique, but I cannot be sure.

This Ongandu was quite a character, and he did insult the police officers in his broken English. Still, that was no excuse for them to beat the hell out of him, the way they did. When they were finished with him, he was all bloody and lay in that cell moaning for hours. I did shout myself hoarse pleading for them to get a doctor, but nobody bothered even to come down to the holding cell. It must have been just before dawn when I first heard him chanting his chant. I did not understand what he was saying and did not recognize the language he was singing in. His eyes were shinning in a strange way as he sang, and he used his hand to keep an intense beat on his thigh.

The mixture of his deep voice and the steady intense beat was mesmerizing, it gave a definite aura of sadness and futility, and it was as if he was enveloped in it, and it was slowly emanating outwards from him. I know because I felt it deep inside my bones. I could see that he was getting weaker and weaker. At one point I asked him to rest and save his strength. My recollection is somewhat hazy, but I think he looked at me and said something like 'I forgive you brother, I forgive them all, but the Great Matu will not forgive... still I try...' and he continued with his sad song.

I must have dozed off for some time, because when I woke up, I could see that Ongandu was lying there on that cold floor of the cell motionless. I understand that the police report stated that he died of natural causes, an acute sudden drop in blood pressure, but I know that Ongandu was beaten to death that night, and I also know that Ongandu knew he was dying when he sang his last song.

Next day I left New Orleans, never to return. That was the same day the city was hit by hurricane Katarina.

I know it sounds crazy, but I still wonder if the city could have been spared its harsh punishment if the Great Matu had accepted Ongandu's appeal.

The Grand Mufti of Paris

Inside the Palace of Light where the Grand Mufti's office was located in central Paris, not far from Avenue Zulfiqar, there was frantic activity. The year was 2001, and the Islamic world covering three quarters of the globe was getting set for the greatest Eid, that which celebrated every year the anniversary of the glowing victory by the armies of the faithful at Poitiers led by the Great Abdel Rahman in 110Hijri (732AD), when Europe was conquered in the name of Islam and Allah's benevolence was introduced to the infidels in the North.

This year's Eid promised to be quite special as the last remnants of fundamentalist Christian terrorism were close to being eliminated. Fundamentalist had resurfaced in recent decades in parts of the New Continent (across the great ocean), Northern and Eastern Europe. Their terrorist activities representing the obstinate refusal by small groups to accept the fact that living as Christians in Dar Al Islam (the House of Islam) necessitated the payment of special taxes, and exclusion from certain privileges allowed only to the faithful.

The Department of Salah El Din (the Righteousness of Religion) also known as the DSD had been pursuing these criminal groups for decades. As per standard practice, when caught, these lost elements were of course subjected to years of 'treatment' leading to the expungence of evil from their souls.

Paris, the city of light, had been for centuries now the political and religious center of the Islamic world. The great Azhar University in the center of the city, casting the light of faith to the remotest corners of the world. What worried Sahib El Fadila (His Piousness) Imam Nour El Din, the Grand Mufti, was the disturbing reports from senior DSD agents that a particular group of Christians scientists had apparently been conducting secret research in temporal physics, with the aim of creating a time machine.

What was science fiction a few decades ago was now apparently science fact. How this group of Christian scientists were able to conduct their research for years without attracting the attention of the DSD was a mystery, and His Piousness was intent on punishing those responsible for this glaring lack of diligence. But first all attention must be directed at stopping these terrorists before they complete their satanic project. They had apparently disappeared just before the DSD scooped to make the arrests. Their whereabouts were not known and a huge reward of 20 million Dinars was offered for any information leading to their capture.

A few days before Eid His Piousness was extremely agitated and worried when he received the latest DSD report. The scientists had been cornered in a remote town in Northern Europe, and before they could be captured they blew themselves up along with all their research notes and equipment. A thorough forensic investigation had revealed that one of the scientists was missing, a young woman. There was also evidence that a machine of sorts was destroyed in the explosion. Was this the 'time machine' that they had been constructing? The evidence was not conclusive. But a digital dial attached to the machine read 732, quite disturbing.

Moreover, the DSD agents found evidence at the scene of a container stolen a few months ago from a medical research laboratory in London where research on influenza was being conducted. A particularly virulent strain of the influenza virus was kept in the missing container. Strange information indeed. While the Grand Mufti was relieved that this group had finally been tracked down and destroyed along with their nefarious machine, he could not help but feeling slightly uneasy about the results of the investigation. Where was the missing woman, and did she intend to spoil the Eid celebrations by exposing innocent people to this virus. Many questions with no answers.

A few days later on the morning of the Eid, September 11, 2001, the Grand Mufti woke up early. He was still in Paris, but in a little apartment on Rue Monsieur le Prince. He was a history professor and was having difficulties recovering from a night of heavy drinking. He was late for a lecture that he was scheduled to give later that day to his students at the Sorbonne. It was one of his favourite lectures. The topic was simply what would have happened had the armies of Islam prevailed at the battle of Poitiers. A battle that ended in annihilation of the Muslim army. One of the reasons of the great victory by the Christian army under Charles Martel was of course the flu epidemic that hit the Muslims a few days before the battle.

Professor Jean Claude always ended his lecture with the joke 'had the Muslims won, who knows, I could have been now the Grand Mufti of Paris... ha-ha.'

The Doll and the Angel of Death

Mustafa the 'Prince' as he was known to his friends was a content man. He drove his own taxi, a 1985 1600cc Russian Lada, a model known as the Tank among Cairo cabbies because of its extra hard body and chassis, well suited to withstand the potholes and bumps of Cairo streets and the inevitable fender benders that form part of driving in the chaotic Cairo traffic, which has been rightly called the world's largest village. His taxi was his life and he called it '*El Arrousa*' the doll, and she was heavily made up with many decorations, even with fake fur and a toy leopard on the back window that moved its head up and down with every bump on the road, and shone bright red when Mustafa hit the brakes.

But that was not the only reason for Mustafa's contentment. He had found the right rhythm to life. He drove a late shift starting at midnight and returning home to Imbaba, one of the larger districts of Cairo on the West bank of the Nile, at around 8 am. Another driver took over at 9 am for the day shift, and they shared the day shift proceeds. This allowed Mustafa to sleep for a few hours, wake up in time for lunch and then sit at his favourite café to play cards and bagammon until the early evening, then he would drop by home for a couple of hours, check on his wife and his four children and then take *El Arrousa* out. First he would pass by a hashish *ghorza* where he would smoke a couple of water pipe tobacco loads laced with hash, exchange the latest jokes with his fellow *hashasheen* and then start his shift. He liked to drive in Cairo at night.

Mustafa considered Cairo to be two cities, a messy, noisy and dust filled day version, which he loathed, and a princess that shone with a million lights well into the night which he adored. One fateful night business was slow, apart from two drunk tourists that he picked up from a Pyramids Road night club and took to the Semeramis hotel, he was stuck with a series of short fares. Around 3 am he was cruising in Giza when he was hailed by an old man with a huge white beard, dressed in a white flowing *gallabiya* that covered all his body including his hand. His head was also covered with a white turban. He stopped, *'get in Haj'* he said, and the old man got into the front seat beside him. *'Where to'* he asked, and the old man gave him directions, turning right, then left then right again, in what seemed to be an endless sequence of turns taking him deep into the heart of Giza's poorer district, along dark narrow streets, deserted at this late hour.

In one of the streets, Mustafa saw a solitary young man who hailed his taxi. '*Do you mind if we pick him up Haj*' he asked. The old man sitting beside him nodded his consent. The young man got into the back seat, '*thank you, I want to go to the airport please*' he told Mustafa. '*No problem, we'll drop the Haj first and then I will take you to the airport*', Mustafa replied.

What do you mean, what Haj? asked the young man. *The Haj right here* Mustafa said pointing to the old man in the front seat. '*What is wrong with you, are you stoned or what, there is no one sitting there... the seat is empty*', the young man shouted. Mustafa was starting to get angry at this point. '*Who are you calling stoned you son of dog he shouted back, get out of the car...*' The young man got out of the car shaking his head, '*you stoned son of a crazed woman*' he called after Mustafa as the taxi drove away.

The old man looked at Mustafa, with a sad smile on his face. '*My son no one can see me except you*'. Mustafa looked at him, '*what do you mean*' he asked. '*I am Azraeel, the angel of death come to take your soul*' the old man said in a deep solemn voice. Mustafa stopped the car and stared at the old man...He could barely make out his face in the darkness only the imposing beard. Mustafa was terrified, so this was the end he thought, to die alone in the early hours of the morning... in an alleyway in Giza of all places. He will never see his wife and children again, he felt tears coming to his eyes. The old man looked at him with pity *'I am afraid I have to take you my son, your hour has come, and what is written must pass. But I can give you ten minutes to pray to Allah at the mosque there at the end of this street. Ask HIM to have mercy on your soul perhaps he will spare you and give you another chance at life... a better life... HE is in the beginning and the end, the all Merciful and Compassionate...'*. Mustafa was crying now, tears flowing down his face, th..tha..thank you he stuttered.

Mustafa got out of the car, and ran into the mosque. He started praying, beseeching Allah to forgive him for spending so much money on hashish depriving his family for his own pleasure, for many other sins that he had committed in his life... the prostitutes he occasionally picked up and slept with, the petty swindles he sometimes made... He shuddered, knowing that he will soon face the torture of the grave, when he will have to account for all his sins before two unforgiving horrifying angels... and he was terrified... He kept looking at his watch... the ten minutes passed like a few seconds, he felt all life draining from his limbs, he was getting weaker. He sat down on the straw mat on the floor of the mosque, knowing that he was dying, he kept repeating the oath *'I swear that there is no God but Allah, and Mohammed (PPBH) is his slave and messenger'*.

After a while Mustafa noticed that he was not dead. Did Azraeel decide to spare him after all? He walked out of the mosque and looked around. *El Aroussa* was gone. Where was she where was Azraeel, he wondered. The Sheikh of the mosque who was preparing for dawn prayers saw Mustafa standing there in front of the mosque, looking dazed. *'What is it my son'*, he asked. *'I am looking for Azraeel and my taxi'*, Mustafa replied. *'May Allah preserve us the poor man is demented'* the Sheikh muttered to himself. He took Mustafa by the hand and said *'come inside and pray to Allah that He may show you the way.'*.

The Police Sergeant who took Mustafa's statement later that morning at Giza Police Station assured him that he was the victim of a couple of con artists out to steal his car. Mustafa never believed this. He was certain that the ten minutes of prayer had saved his life. For him, the price was high, his beloved *Arrousa* (which was never found), but still for him it was worth it. He led a changed life from that day onwards, he stopped smoking hashish, was more generous to his family, and while he continued to drive taxis (now working for others).

Mustafa never took the night shift again.

The Bus on Avenida Cordoba

It was 1976, he was standing on the sidewalk of Avenida Cordoba downtown Madrid, in front of the impressive International Student Center where he had been attending a class in Spanish. He was still thinking about the teacher's comment that Franco should always be referred to as '*Generalismo*'. Franco had been dead for two years and yet he still cast a heavy shadow on the land.

Deep in his thoughts he started to step down to cross the avenue, for some inexplicable reason, perhaps a sixth sense that only comes into play at crucial moments, he looked to his left and froze in mid air, a huge bus whizzed by missing him by inches, he could feel the wind on his face as the bus sped by. That was close, very close, he thought.

A fraction of a second more and I would have certainly died, right here in Madrid, aged twenty. So, everything that comes now in life, is a bonus. The thought should have cheered him, instead he felt lost and depressed.

The near bus accident preoccupied him for a long time. He could not help but feel the sheer arbitrariness of it all. Death, cessation of existence was always there a fraction of a second away. How many people died just because they did not have that fateful fraction of a second to act, or freeze or whatever. He became obsessed with the idea of chaos in the universe. The theories of uncertainty and randomness that apparently informed everything in the cosmos. As a physicist his main area of research was the nature of time. Einstein's genius was that he dared to think the unthinkable, he theorized that time itself was relative. A second for X is not necessarily a second for Y, it all depends on the relative speed of X to Y. Time dilates and space expands. Einstein's theory was confirmed through many experiments. Quantum physics then opened the whole uncertainty principle, with particles acting in unpredictable ways, popping up in the future and the past and even passing through solid matter.

He worked hard, and although he was not exceptional and did not really contribute much to physics, he was a competent teacher and reached the respectable position of professor at the university. He married young and had three children, and in time several grandchildren. On the whole he was satisfied with his life. Although his concern about randomness, uncertainty and the arbitrariness of life, the concern that started on that sidewalk in Madrid many years ago, stayed with him. One might even say it gnawed slowly at him. He could never really exorcise that demon.

Later in his life, much later, when he was in his late 80s, he became a resident of an old people's home. His wife had died some years before, and as he was never really very close to his children, he did not mind too much the Home. One evening he was sitting in his room rummaging through an old tin box that had been brought to him that day by his eldest son. His son had found the box in a basement closet at his house. He remembered that he did have such a box so many years ago, in his early twenties, even before he got married.

He laughed in delight as he saw some pictures of himself as a school boy in uniform, his tie as usual all askew. He then found a picture of some students standing before the International Student Center in Madrid. Oh yes there was no mistaking the old building with its impressive, beautiful architecture. He looked closely at the picture, he of course had his reading glasses on, but still had some difficulty making out the details. He got his handy magnifier and peered at the picture. Yes, that was Avenida Cordoba alright.

There was a bus stopped at a strange angle in the middle of the avenue. One of the students was pointing at the bus. Some students were running towards the bus, others had their hands on their faces. He looked at the bus in the picture, there was something lying under the middle of the bus, it looked like some sack. He squinted and peered closer at the picture. No that was not a sack, it was a human form, grotesquely crumpled.

He felt the blood drain from his face as he sat in his room in the old people's home. He knew with absolute certainty to whom the body under the bus belonged. It was a young twenty-year-old student, it was himself dead all these years ago under the wheels of the bus on Avenida Cordoba.

He laughed softly to himself and closed his eyes, so he did get his bonus after all, but not in the way he thought he had. He was still there frozen in front of that bus about to die, yet in his mind he had lived over 68 years. Lived these years fully, all in a small fraction of a second. There was fairness after all, and the theory of relativity applied. No one died before their time. Now his time was up, what remained of his fractional second was about to be consumed, hence the message from his mind to prepare himself. He was ready, and still smiling he opened his eyes and saw the bus in front of him.

He died instantly on impact.

Miami Rock

Alexandria of the 1960s is long gone, Ibrahim thought as he walked along the Corniche by the raging sea. Life as he knew it in the 1960s was gone. He remembered the long three months vacations his family used to take. Packing the small Fiat 1100 with all the summer's needs, umbrellas, beach chairs etc. Going from Cairo to Alexandria along the Agricultural Road that cut through the Nile Delta. The trip used to take close to 4 hours, with a stop at *Burg Al Munifia* for the famous pancakes.

Now people can no longer afford lengthy vacations, the hectic pace of life where the Egyptian middle class is clambering after all the glitzy consumer goods, only allows people quick weekends, zipping to Alex along the now expanded four lane desert road. Yet here he was in May at Alexandria, the waves of Cairenes that would descend on the city during the summer months have not yet begun, and the city was relatively quiet.

All his life Ibrahim has been careful, although his ex-wife would sometimes call it cowardice. He had always towed the line. Now a famous journalist, and editor in chief, of a leading governmental daily newspaper, he could afford all the luxuries of the good life. His income from the commissions on advertising alone was monthly in the tens of thousands.

But Ibrahim was faced with a crisis of sorts. Samia Amer, a young idealistic journalist at the paper had uncovered some large-scale corruption at the Ministry of Tourism. Naturally she had to be silenced. For some perverse reason, he had always liked this young woman, perhaps because she represented everything in a journalist that he was not, an honest and serious approach, and the struggle to expose the truth. Now he was asked, in no subtle terms, to cook up some charge against her, so that she could be threatened with expulsion or even criminal proceedings. The carrot of course would be a big promotion if she could just forget about the story. In short, the usual recipe to turn an honest journalist into a tame one, owned by those in power.

Ibrahim was in Alexandria attending a seminar, when all these nostalgic memories of his childhood came back. He could not understand why he was so disturbed by this Samia Amer matter. He was walking along the Corniche at Alexandria's Miami Beach. He sat on the balustrade, as he used to do many years ago, and stared out at the sea, which was quite rough with high waves. He could see the famous Miami Rock several hundred meters into the sea.

Many years ago when he was a teenager and spent his summers here, kids who were brave enough would swim out to the Rock. This was quite a dare, as the current was fierce, and the waves could easily smash swimmers against the rock. Over the years several people drowned while swimming to the Rock. Although he was a good swimmer, he remembered that he could never take up this dare. His friends during the summer would eventually all prove their courage by swimming out to the Rock. He became an object of their ridicule because he could never muster enough courage to take that swim. The girls were polite, but he could always sense their contempt. Shit, perhaps if he had taken that swim so many years ago, he would now have been more like Samia, a different person, a real journalist. He went down to the beach and stood for a long time staring at the Rock. Then he took out his mobile phone and called the paper. He gave clear instructions to his deputy regarding Samia Amer. He then took off his clothes, and waded in swimming slowly against the waves out towards the Rock.

Next morning, all the daily newspapers carried the story of Ibrahim's tragic death. He had apparently drowned while taking an early morning swim in Alexandria. While no one mentioned suicide, this assumption could be read between the lines in most of the published reports. There was mention of his recent divorce and his lengthy treatment abroad for depression and alcoholism.

A few days later Ibrahim's newspaper carried an important front-page story written by Samia Amer describing the resounding success of the Government's new policy to develop tourism in the North Coast. Samia Amer was promoted shortly thereafter and had a brilliant career at the paper.

The Fatwa

After so many years, the events that took place in the small village of K near Aleppo are no longer so clear to me, and I would not like to give the wrong impression of what happened, but there is a question that preys on my mind, and telling the story may help me find the true answer.

I was a young boy attending *Kottab* school, and our teacher, the Imam of the mosque was a tall, bearded man with a strong face and a voice that went well with it, full of certainty and confidence, He was quite knowledgeable in all the four schools of Islam. As the only religious figure in the area, he officiated at marriages, funerals, and all other matters where the intricacies of our faith were needed. In that capacity he also gave many *fatwas* (religious theological opinions) to people who came from near and far to ask questions and enquire about how they could live their lives in line with the straight and narrow path decreed by the Holy Koran and the teachings of our beloved Prophet (PBUH). These *fatwas* were often given at the small village mosque after the evening *isha* prayers.

It was so many years ago, but I still remember. I was sitting in the mosque with all the other pupils, boys and girls and some of the villagers. The evening prayer had been finished and the Imam was telling us a story from the dawn of Islam. *Om* (mother of) Mohamed, the wife of the man who used to be the village butcher, but was now retired, a very old woman, she must have been over eighty

81

years of age, walked into the mosque and sat down in the back with the rest of the women and girls. At one point she asked the Imam for a *fatwa*. She asked him if she would be allowed to divorce her husband after a marriage of 65 years.

A silence fell, and I could see the Imam's face contort in confusion. Why he asked her would she want a divorce after so many years. She told him that she heard on the radio, the grand Mufti of Syria say that marriage was a sacred bond that would continue even after death, and that married couples would remain married in heaven. The Imam nodded his head and confirmed that this was true. The woman looked down and then said '*ya sidna al sheikh (o venerable sheikh)* I have served my husband in silence for 65 years, I have been faithful and obedient, and I have borne many hardships and pain for him, but I cannot bear the thought of this lasting for eternity. I want to be absolved of this marriage before I die.'

Perhaps for the first time I saw some uncertainty on the face of our Imam. He stayed silent for a while, and then told the woman that he will research her question and that he will have an answer for her after one week. The following week, the Imam virtually disappeared, he was so engrossed in researching the *fatwa*, that he hardly left his home. The following week, the matter had become quite known in the region, and hundreds of people crammed into our little mosque to hear the Imam's *fatwa* to *Om* Mohammed. After the *isha* prayers *Om* Mohammed walked in and sat at the back. The Imam looked at her and said: 'my sister I have studied all the important sources in search for an answer to your question. His face hardened, and he whispered 'who are you to question God's will? What is written is written, and we all have to bear it... there are no grounds for divorce in your case.'

There was a great silence in the mosque, The old woman looked at him, and I can still see her expression of utmost despair that seemed to have added many lines to her already wrinkled face. She stood up and walked out of the mosque without another word. I looked at the Imam that moment and I could swear that he had some tears in his eyes, even though he quickly stood up and left the mosque.

A few days later we learned that *Om* Mohammed had died in her sleep. The funeral was a sad event with all the village attending. The Imam recited many verses from the Holy Book, but I could detect a quiver in his voice, and his face was like a mask difficult to read, What I remember is that shortly after these events the Imam stopped teaching at the *kottab*, and a few weeks later he even stopped leading prayers at the mosque. He withdrew from all religious activities and, he a learned man, was content to live the life of a simple shepeard.

He moved away from the village and took his sheep to the mountains. The tides and waves of life carried me to many places, and I ended up as a teacher in a primary school in Damascus, but despite my travels I maintained a habit of visiting my village once a year during the *Biram Eid*. It was an opportunity to see childhood friends and relatives and participate in the ritual slaughter of the lamb in deference to Allah's mercy in sparing *sayidna* (our master) Ibrahim the horror of sacrificing his own son *sayidna* Ismail.

About twenty years ago during one of my visits I enquired about the Imam and was told that he still lived in the mountains. I sought out my old teacher. I took my car up the mountain roads and found him. He was much older, and his beard was now all white, but what struck me most was his face. It no longer bore that hard look of certainty. His voice also seemed to be gentler. He was quite hospitable and invited me to share a modest lunch of cheese and hard bread. When I finally got the courage, just before I left, to ask him why he decided to stop being an Imam, he was silent for a while, and then he whispered: 'my brother...there is only now, the moment... and it lasts for eternity... this is heaven and hell...'

His words rang in my head as I drove back, and with it the question had the Imam lost his faith, or had he found it at last?

Shidwan

After so many years I am confident that I have earned the right to tell my story. I am sure it will come as a shock to all those who know me, but I have no regrets. I have served the people my two countries faithfully and my efforts when I was Prime Minister have after all brought peace to this vibrant and troubled corner of our world. I hope I do not sound too pompous, but modesty was never my forte.

I was an Egyptian (I guess I have always remained one) specialized in the Hebrew language. In 1968 I had just graduated and been appointed as a research assistant at the Faculty of Arts at Cairo University. I was of course conscripted into the Army right after graduation. By 1969 in the aftermath of the 1967 *naksa* (catastrophe), the Egyptians were still fighting, and the so called 'war of attrition' was at its height. The Egyptian Army had a listening post on Shidwan a small uninhabited island in the Red Sea, one of hundreds of such island scattered south of Sinai.

The island of Shidwan was shaped like a giant elephant. Sophisticated equipment (by the standards of the time) was deployed there to listen to Israeli military radio traffic. As a Hebrew specialist, I was posted there, part of a platoon under the command of a young lieutenant. If I recall correctly his name was Hamza, he hailed from Alexandria and was an ardent Zamalek supporter, the arch enemy of Al Ahly, the football team that I supported (why do I still remember these details after so many years?).

One of our latrines was nestled between two rock outcrops on top of the Elephant's head, giving those squatting there to do their business a wonderful view of the island and the clear blue waters of the Red Sea. Because of this we nick named this latrine the 'Throne'. Israeli military intelligence archives (which I later naturally had full access to) show that the listening post was detected sometime in late December 1969, and a raid was planned to wipe it out.

The raid took place in early January 1970. It was a bloody battle. The Egyptian Army still holds its head high when Shidwan is mentioned. Not unlike Iwo Jima, a small defending force gave a vastly superior attacking force extremely stiff and heroic resistance. The Egyptians went down fighting to the last man, some say to the last bullet, taking with them many Israelis. I was there so I know.

It so happened that the night before the raid we had opened some cans of sardines, and I was unlucky to get a serious case of diarrhea. I spent most of the night squatting on the Throne on top of the Elephant's Head. This was what saved my life. It was a moonless night, and the raid started around three a.m. in pitch darkness, with Israeli Special Forces landing at various points of the island. I will not go into the details of the battle, it lasted for several hours and was desperate and merciless from both sides. I saw most of it from my perch up at the Throne. I took a few shots now and then at the enemy (yes Israelis were my enemies then) and it was very difficult to make out friend from foe.

Given the rocky nature of the island and its numerous well protected caves, the Israelis had decided on an unconventional approach. They attacked in darkness relying on close combat. At one point I remember I was grabbed from behind and a knife was stuck into my side, I was certain that I was as good as dead, the pain was terrible, and I could feel the knife being withdrawn for another stab.

I still recall the moment of the explosion. A grenade went off a few meters behind me and killed the man who was so intent on taking my life. He took most of the blast as I was partly shielded by his body. What irony, in the act of killing me instead of taking my life he gave me a new one. I was blown off my feet. He was lying close to me, his head a bloody pulp.

I do not know exactly what prompted me, but I knew instinctively that this was a night where no quarter would be asked for or given, and that if I was to live to see the dawn, I must somehow put on his uniform, or what was left of it. This I did in the darkness. I dressed him in my own uniform and rolled him down the slope of the hill forming the Elephant's ear. In addition to the wound at my side, my face was also bleeding, I had caught some shrapnel. I felt faint and sat on the ground with my back against the side of the Throne, and while I was not a religious person, and was perhaps a Muslim by name and not practice, I instinctively repeated the two testimonies of Islam that traditionally need to be uttered when a person's soul is to depart on its journey back to its maker. That is the last thing I remember from that night.

I recovered consciousness at an Israeli field military hospital in Sinai. Apparently, I had been muttering in Hebrew, and with the uniform I was naturally taken to be a wounded Israeli. In fact, my face had been disfigured to such an extent that they could not tell that I was not the man who shielded me from the blast. I told them that I could not remember anything, and this was then attributed to amnesia caused by the blast. I underwent extensive plastic surgery and the doctors finally managed to put together a new face for me. I was discharged from the army as a decorated veteran.

It never occurred to me to go back to Egypt, even after Sadat's initiative and the peace treaty with Egypt. I felt that I had died in Shidwan (perhaps I did) and was reborn as an Israeli. I felt that I had an opportunity to do something worthwhile. When I went into politics joining the Labour Party ticket, I knew exactly what my ultimate objective was. After a long and tough political career I was finally elected as head of the Party and became Prime Minister more than fifty years after Shidwan.

The peace treaty that I signed with the Palestinians was my crowning achievement, and it is something that I am proud of. Some say I gave away too much, others say that I did not give enough, but I tell you that I did exactly what was needed to stop the bloodshed. After so many years I am still amazed how it all started, with a small can of sardines that kept me up on that Throne on the Elephant's head.

I am not a religious man, but if I were, I would say that God not only works in mysterious ways, but he also has a hell of a sense of humour.

Shalom.

The Long Goodbye

The village of LB was one of the many so-called 'touristic' villages built on the Mediterranean coast North of Egypt, stretching from Alexandria to the East to El Saloom on the Libyan border to the West. These touristic villages in some cases boasted extremely expensive large villas with private pools. Well to do middle class Egyptians strived, as a sign of prestige, to own units on this Northern Coast, referred to simply as the 'Coast'. They flocked to the 'Coast' in their millions over the course of every summer. Spending weekends and holidays on the beaches.

LB was one of the quieter villages with nice big villas and a wonderful beach that stretched for close to two kilometers. However, the reason why K, a retired banker in his early sixties, bought a villa at LB was the promenade that followed the line of the beach. For K a daily brisk evening walk was the key to good health. He immediately saw the long promenade at LB as the ideal venue for his evening walks. After sunset when the turquoise sea turned into a wine-dark sea as Homer would describe it, the promenade was lit by some two hundred electric lanterns, one imbedded every ten meters or so into the body of a short half a meter wall on the Northern side of the promenade. The Wall served to protect the promenade from the sand blowing off the beach.

The beach itself, with its fine white sand, stretched for about 50 meters North of that wall all the way to where the waves broke on the sand in their incessant never ending rhythm, as if trying in vain to regain the land that was lost from the oceans millions of years ago. When the promenade was lit every evening after sunset, the lanterns cast a beautiful light and K sitting in his balcony could make out the feet of the residents of the Village who took evening strolls along the promenade as they passed in front of the lanterns.

K preferred late evening walks when the promenade was empty and would usually begin his walks at around 11 pm. His villa was close to the Eastern edge of the Village and he would walk all the way the Western edge and back, a walk of close to four kilometers. This would take him on average, with his brisk pace, about fifty minutes to complete. K had never married and had resigned himself many years ago to live alone with his books, music and telescopes. He was an amateur astronomer and photographer and quite well travelled.

K was not a religious man; in fact, he had serious doubts about the existence of God. The misery that prevailed human existence and the myriad of different beliefs that caused people to butcher each other, all contributed to his deep skepticism. Despite all of his doubts, he still wondered at some of the mysteries of the Universe. For example, why did the big bang occur? In addition, where did it occur? Regarding death, as was the wont of most people, when he was young, he never really considered his own mortality. It was when he grew older that he started to resign himself to the inevitable end that would befall him, as it did all people since the dawn of time.

K did not believe in an afterlife. For him with death comes total darkness and a nothingness, his body rotting and decomposing reverting back to inanimate matter. His mind would be extinguished like a candle in the wind; nothing would be left of that flame of life, of matter conscious of itself and the Universe. He thought it was a cruel fate that befell us humans, destined to become aware, to have a mind, only to know that in a short, ever so short, a time, we will become nothing again.

One night K was walking along the promenade alone as usual towards the Western edge of the Village when he glimpsed a young woman sitting on one of the few stone benches on the beach placed on the Northern side of the promenade. She was young, perhaps 25 years old or thereabouts. She was pretty with long dark hair. He could barely make out her shape in the darkness, but she had a well-proportioned body. Quite attractive. She wore a sleeveless summer dress.

As K walked by, he muttered a hesitant 'good evening'. He was always weary of imposing on other people's private moments. He was pleasantly surprised when she answered in a loud cheerful voice 'and good evening to you Sir'. The 'Sir' stung a little, as K understood that it underlined the age difference between them. He passed her by and completed his walk to the Western end of the village.

On his way back she was gone. Next evening, she was there again. They exchanged another set of 'good evenings. The third night when he saw her sitting on the bench he decided to stop and talk to her. After their usual exchange of pleasantries, he asked her what she was doing each evening sitting on the bench. She told him that she liked to sit in the dark under the stars and listen to the sound of the waves as they met the beach. They talked for a little while longer and then he resumed his walk.

It became a habit of K every night to stop and talk briefly to the girl. He became impressed with her way of thinking. When she asked him about the stars and what they were made of, he found that he very much enjoyed explaining to her some of the basics of astronomy. After a few of weeks during which they had a conversation every evening, one night when they met, she told him that she would be leaving the LB next morning 'to return home'.

K was surprised at the disappointment that he suddenly felt, before this moment he was not aware of how much he liked talking to the girl. Their evening talks had become something he looked forward to every day. He bid her a safe trip and asked her if they could again. At this question, she gave him an enigmatic look, with some sadness in it, stood up without speaking and walked away.

At the end of the season, as usual K was one of the last residents of LB to pack-up and leave. As he did every year,

K passed by the manager who oversees all the services at LB to say goodbye and have a cup of tea. He as curious about the girl, so he asked the manager about her, wanting to know the Villa at which she stayed.

When K posed his question, the manager gave a start and went very pale. He remained silent for a while, not looking at K. Then he looked at K and asked him to describe this 'girl'. After K described her, the manager sighed and told K that the girl was not real and that should forget all about her. 'What do you mean not real?' shouted K, who suddenly became quite agitated, sensing that something was quite wrong. The Manager shook his head and told K that according to local superstition among the Bedouin tribes in the area, death itself in the guise of a beautiful young woman would sometimes show itself to people who are about to die. They regarded this as a one of the '*karamat*' or miraculous events that sometimes take place when the thin veil between life and death is set aside.

K smiled in contempt and told the manager that this was complete rubbish and that an educated man such as the manager should not believe in such nonsense. K drove off from LB convinced that the manager for some reason had concocted this whole story about local beliefs. He did not imagine what his motives might have been, but he thought that perhaps the manager was himself sweet on the girl and sensed that K, notwithstanding his age, might be a rival. He dismissed these thoughts from his head and became determined to find girl by any means. Deep inside him, he was sure that they would meet again.

Later that same day the news networks in Egypt reported a major accident on the desert road linking the Capital with the North Coast.

There were a number of fatalities, including a retired banker.

A Brief History of Ideas

In the beginning there was nothing (there is a lot of philosophical debate about this 'nothing' can there be 'nothing' without there ever being 'something'), anyway then there was something (that is certain). How this something came to be is also subject to some debate, whether it was a big bang, a small bang, divine will etc. Anyway, fast forward a few billion years, and we have a multitude of objects hurtling through at least one universe, which seems to be expanding from one point of origin.

Some of these objects are called stars, and there are many billions of these stars clustered together in things that are called galaxies. There are billions of galaxies. In one of these galaxies, which includes billions of stars, there is a medium sized star called the sun, or sol. There are things orbiting around sol, these includes large chunks of matter/rocks called planets.

The third rock from the sun is called Earth. Fast forward a few billion years, Earth is now surrounded by gases, called the atmosphere. Earth itself is liquid on the surface. That liquid at one point is called the primordial soup. Why soup, I guess because it has many ingredients that are being somehow cooked slowly.

Now some of the things in the soup start to connect with other things, and to divide. This is called the miracle of life. Apparently, these very small organisms (things after all) start to multiply, and in doing so over billions of years, they start to take new shapes. Fast forward two more billion years, and there is land on earth, and some of these things have left the soup pot and are now 'living' as well on land and in the air. These things have now taken a multitude of shapes and designs. They are as 'things' of course part of everything else, and they combine with all other things, devouring and being devoured, and when dead they take other forms of things.

Fast forward a few hundred million years, and we find that some of these things are quite large compared to others, these are called dinosaurs. The dinosaurs dominate other things, until at one point they disappear. Why did this happen, there are many theories, a comet striking Earth is the prevailing one.

A few million years later we find that some of these things are moving on two feet, they are called bipeds. Some of them have unusually large brains and have developed the ability to hold other things with their upper limbs, using hands and opposable thumbs. Hundreds of thousands of years later, one type of these bipeds becomes dominant, with an even bigger brain and is more flexibility in using hands. These things are called homo sapiens.

Primitive tools are developed. At one point something incredible happened, a form of sound communication was invented, and homo sapiens communicate using a variety of sounds. This is called language. Different sounds are allocated to other things, to feelings, to everything. Ideas are born, and eventually as language developed, all these other things could only be thought of through language and ideas. They become a part of language and cease to exist in the minds of homo sapiens outside of language. This is how the things called homo sapiens lost contact with all other things in the universe and became trapped in the language they created.

Eventually homo sapiens started to think of themselves not as things, but as beings, superior (superiority is one of the ideas they developed) to all other things. The power of language was such, that they created some things that only lived in ideas and language such as unicorns, dragons, and magical beings. They sought to subordinate the whole universe to their will. Other means of communicating language were devised, these included various forms of writing and symbols. The universe itself became part of language, of thoughts and ideas. Some of them expressed this as the divine will devised by a superior being, in whose form they were shaped. Others even suggested that nothing really existed outside of ideas in their minds.

Yet homo sapiens were persistently nagged by two ideas, life and death. For them death was the end of ideas, when the brain no longer functioned, what they called 'brain death'. They could not tolerate this. Some of them banished death through the idea of 'ever-lasting life'. Others sought immortality through the idea of continuity of the species and survival of ideas. Pushed relentlessly by ideas that were becoming more and more complicated, homo sapiens continued to devour and use all other things at an accelerating and increasingly more efficient pace. Ideas such as time, the future, destiny, love, happiness, exploration, honour, glory and achievement continued to drive them.

All this came to an end when a very small thing, called a microbe evolved, and attacked that part of homo sapiens' brain used to process language. This phenomenon they called a 'disease', a world pandemic, and it spread throughout Earth, carried by the water and air affecting all homo sapiens. As a result of this disease homo sapiens lost the ability to use language.

With the death of language came the death of ideas, and homo sapiens isolation with the universe and all other things was ended and they became one with all things again. But as things they did not last long. Without language and thought they could no longer use their external tools, and their bodies, hands feet and teeth were no longer sufficient for them to survive.

In a few hundred years they were wiped out, eventually destroyed by other things.

Charmed I am Sure

It was just past 6 am and the streets had this pre-dawn aura that gives a sense of magic in the air. The streetlamps cast a hazy yellowy light... and the trees were large shadows looming in the dark. I was out in my track suit ready to start my brisk one-hour daily walk in the streets of Zamalek, of late my main form of exercise.

At that time of the morning, one could still see a few stars and the hint of the coming day in the East, and sometimes even the moon. I started along Gezira Street moving south towards the Southwest gate of the Gezira Sporting Club, that vestige of ancient colonialist British rule in Egypt. As was my habit I was trying to focus on the beautiful trees on both sides of the street.

The Island of Zamalek, now smack in the center of Cairo is a real botanical garden. Many of the trees were imported by Khedive Ismail in the 19th century. There were huge eucalyptus trees, pine trees, India rubber trees and at least three types of palm trees.

The street was deserted, and as sometimes happens on my walks I glimpsed another lone walker some distance away. In the early morning half-light, he looked like a faraway ethereal being, like a ghost. We were moving in opposite directions and the distance between us was closing.

As he approached, I could start to make out his clothes and appearance. He had a blue sports jacket on and white shorts. The jacket had two white lines down the middle. What struck me as he came even closer was the colour of his hair. It was greenish brown. I was surprised but not overly so. I used to have greenish brown hair myself back when I was an engineering student at Cairo University. I used to swim nearly every day at the Lido pool at the Gezira club, and the amount of chemicals including chloroform they put in the water at that time in the 1970s was totally unregulated. They probably meant well, but for a couple of years I did have greenish brown hair.

This early morning walker did bring back memories. In fact, when I was a student, I also had a blue sports jacket with two white lines down the middle very much like the one worn by the stranger coming towards me. All these thoughts scrambled within my mind in a split second as we walked closer and closer to each other. I started to get an uneasy feeling about this encounter.

As the stranger approached I looked him straight in the face. He was young, in his late teens or early twenties. His was clean shaven with long hair. At least long by Egyptian standards. His eyes were brownish green. He stared back at me as we passed each other. I was perplexed, I felt that

I somehow knew this young man. His face looked oddly familiar...but I could not place him.

I continued walking towards the club gate, preoccupied with the idea that I have seen this young man before but could not remember when and where. I stopped walking for a minute or two, thinking about this. Suddenly in a flash I knew exactly who this young man was. There was no doubt in my mind, even though the idea was totally crazy.

I turned around and looked back towards the direction he had taken. I could barely glimpse him in the half dark. I shouted for him to wait and started running towards him. I do not think he heard me, he was too far away, he continued walking. As my legs hit the pavement running, I wondered at this insane encounter with my younger self. Although the very idea was totally crazy, I was certain that a few minutes ago I had met myself some 35 years ago. I must have been on my way back from my daily swim. Given the greenish hair, I could place the date at sometime between 1974 and 1975.

As I ran hard towards the fast-receding figure, I wondered what I will tell myself. Perhaps I would advise against continuing my studies at the faculty of engineering. Perhaps I could give some investment tips or provide information that would lead to fame and fortune. How would I live my life differently was the question screaming loudly inside my head. Suddenly it dawned on me, if I changed even a very small thing in my life, all that has happened to me over the past 35 years would be different. Perhaps I would never meet my wife and my children would never be born. These were frightening thoughts...

I slowed down. I stopped running and stood there under a huge tree and watched the figure in the green tweed jacket walk away and recede slowly out of my sight. I fought the urge to run after him again and just stood there for a few more minutes.

I turned around and walked back towards the Southwest gate of the Gezira club.

Arzak

Café *El Horiya* (liberty) was as usual quite crowded in the late afternoon. The smoke from the shishas (waterpipes) apple laced tobacco filled the air. Sitting at his usual table, Mahfouz sipped his tea slowly. He could hear the sound of bagammon dice being thrown, the pieces being slammed down and the triumphant calls of Basra! from the card players. The television on a shelf high on the wall at one of the corners of the Café had a popular drama serial on, but nobody could hear anything above the din of the place.

It had been a hard day of work at the Bank where Mahfouz was a *farash* (office boy) serving tea and coffee all day on the executive floor on the seventh floor, and Mahfouz savoured the moment of rest as he let the smoke and noise wash the day's troubles away. Moments like this made life worth living he thought to himself.

Abbas a taxi driver and Mahfouz's friend walked in. As Abbas pulled a chair, Mahfouz could see that he was clearly excited about something. 'Listen Mahfouz' Abbas said in a low voice, 'could you keep a secret?' 'Of course,' replied Mahfouz, 'what is it?' Abbas looked around and bent close to Mahfouz 'the porthole of fate has opened for me *ya sahbi* (my friend).'

Abbas told Mahfouz that he had just driven a man to the airport. An American elderly gentleman who was staying at the Four Seasons hotel. En route the man conversed with Abbas in broken Arabic. Abbas hoping for a big tip started to tell him about how hard life had become with the rising prices, and how he barely made a living for his family out of Aziza his old, battered taxi.

When they got to the airport, the man had apologized for not having local currency and offered him a bill in American currency instead, telling him to keep the change. Abbas looked at the bill, he could see that it had some zeros, and at first, he thought it was a hundred-dollar bill. That was equal to more than ten times the fare in local currency, so he accepted and thanked the man profusely, throwing in a prayer for Allah to *yemer bittak'* (keep your home prosperous). As he was driving back with a passenger from the airport, he looked at the bill again, and only then he realized that it had too many zeros. He was worried and decided to show it to Mahfouz.

Abbas showed the bill to Mahfouz. 'I think it is more than a hundred dollars' Abbas whispered to Mahfouz. Mahfouz looked at the bill and started to laugh. 'This is a million-dollar bill, see it has six zeros. In all my years at the bank I have never heard of such a bill. I think you have been conned my friend.' Abbas' face dropped, and his boisterous excitement evaporated immediately. 'A million dollars, oh black day, the son of a dog tricked me then.'

Mahfouz called the waiter and ordered a lemon juice for his friend to calm his nerves. 'You live and learn Abbas that is the way of the world. Next time be more careful.' They sat in silence for a while, and then Mahfouz suddenly shouted 'I have a great idea. Why don't we sell it to one of the *Saaidi's* (southerners from Upper Egypt) and split the proceeds'. Abbas mulled over the idea in his mind for a while, and then slowly nodded 'good idea but we have to pick our man carefully.'

Al Horiya was right next to *Bab El Hadid* (the iron gate) the main railway station in Cairo, and as such was frequented by passengers who have either just arrived or were waiting for their trains. They watched closely everyone who entered the Café, until they saw a man who from his *galabiya* and head cover was clearly a *Saaidi.* As the man entered, and Abbas and Mahfouz called him over to their table. 'The most chivalrous of people' Abbas told the newcomer when he told them he was from a village close to Qena, a city some six hundred Kilometers south of Cairo.

It turned out the man was a construction labourer who was going later to the airport to fly to Qatar having spent his family's savings to secure a three-year contract. His dream, like every poor Egyptian, was to save enough money to build a small house in his village. 'Well, this is your lucky day' Mahfouz told him. 'You see I have a hundred-dollar bill. It so happens that I am short of cash and cannot wait for the banks to open in the morning. It is worth five hundred and fifty pounds, but I am willing to sell it right now for four hundred only. Mind you Egyptian pounds cannot be exchanged in the Gulf and you will need foreign currency.'

After haggling for a while, the *Saaidi* bought the bill for three hundred pounds and Abbas threw in a free lift to the airport in his taxi. Driving back. Mahfouz looked at Abbas and could feel that his friend felt a little bit guilty. 'That is the way of the world' he told his friend 'it is *arzak* (revenue sent by Allah).' Their mood became lighter, and the two friends laughed out loud when they imagined the *Saaidi's* face as he tried to cash the bill in Qatar.

A week later Mahfouz was sitting at *Al Horiya* in the evening when Abbas walked in. They were sipping their tea, when suddenly Abbas shouted 'look at the television, isn't that the *Saaidi*?' Mahfouz looked at the small screen, and indeed there was a reporter talking to their *Saaidi*. They asked the waiter to raise the volume and walked over closer to the set. It was a news report about a poor Egyptian labourer who cashed a million-dollar bill in Qatar. He was now returning to his village near Qena, a wealthy man.

The two friends looked at each other, and Mahfouz shook his head and said in a quiet voice '*arzak...arzak*'.

The Last Message

The sun is finally setting over the Great Temple and I am the last priest. I sit alone among the ruins of what was once the center of the universe. I am now resigned to the inevitable. I even wonder why I bother to write down these words. Nothing can change what happened and a few words here or there are ultimately meaningless.

Yes, I am talking to you who is now reading the miserable futile reminiscing of an old fool; do not be so arrogant to assume that I write for you, I write for myself and my silent despair.

I still wear my torn robe of the high priesthood, a robe that was once splendid bright red with gold trimmings and jewels and is now a faded bare dull beige. With the death of the Divine so many years ago, I deserve no more. I will now record for the first time the true events that led to the end of Digital Meaning.

Following the destructive Great Holocaust, the one by which stupid humanity destroyed most of the known world, there was born the great new plan. The surviving remnants of humanity, 'the People', numbering only a few hundred thousand, existed in one corner of North America, a region that for some odd twist of fate was spared the fallout that brought to a painful end the lives of all other homo sapiens on this planet.

Fortunately, a giant computer center was located within this region. The computer programmers and technicians managed to keep the system working and to bring back up most of the technical functions required for survival at the same level of civilization attained before the Holocaust.

In the face of the realization that there must be a sublime meaning to human existence, the People, with the guidance of the First Lord, the chief of these technicians, organized and created the Church of Digital Meaning. The priesthood was composed of computer programmers and technicians. The Church, through the giant computer at the heart of the system (the 'Machine'), managed and controlled all aspects of daily life.

Early on, the Church's theologians recognized the need for a benevolent omnipotent divine being, an omniscient entity in the image of man to control the Machine. Humanity needed continuous guidance and interference if it was to avoid yet another holocaust. Thus, some 300 years ago the Divine was born again. The First Divine Lord was the Chief of the founders of our Church, may his divine name shine and echo in the heavens.

In His wisdom the First Divine structured a succession system that would avoid strife and inner fighting within the priesthood. A pure meritocracy.

Upon the departure of the Divine from this material existence to a higher digital existence, His or Her body would be cremated in a most holy ceremony. The successor would be selected from the young priests and priestesses of the Church of Digital Meaning.

Those below the age of 30 would attend at the Great Temple for the divine exams. These were an unbelievably difficult set of physical, spiritual, and mental tests designed by the priesthood to select the strongest and the brightest and most dedicated young man or woman to be elevated to the divine plateau and sit on the divine console.

Our last Divine Mistress started out in the traditional manner. She was elevated, received the holy codes that allowed control of the Machine and assumed Her place at the Holy Console. As the High Priest I alone had the privilege and honour to enter the inner sanctum of the

Great Temple where I could communicate directly with Her Divinity.

The first few years of Her Divine existence went without any extraordinary incidents. We had the occasional need to punish some dissidents here and there. As expected, Her punishment was swift and merciless. Sinners and small communities that strayed from the teachings of the Church were deprived of water purification, heating, and other services necessary to maintain life in the new perpetual winter that followed the Great Holocaust.

Attempts by subversives to move to other communities were repelled by Her flying angels, the drones of death. All such rebellious and deviant communities, as has been the case since the foundation of the Church, were swiftly crushed and annihilated.

The problem started when a small community of about one hundred households submitted a petition to the Church seeking an exemption from the punishment decreed for anyone, outside the Church, who possessed one of the sacred books. All computer programming and technical manuals were of course deemed sacred and restricted to the Church. Otherwise, sinners and deviants may find ways of subverting or sabotaging the Divine will by tampering with the Machine.

The case involved a young boy of 18 who was found by the Digital Inquisition to have possession of an ancient book entitled 'Guide to C++ Programming for Dummies'. The book itself must have been at least 300 years old, and Digital Heaven alone knows how the boy found it. On its face the book was harmless enough, since the programming language to which it referred could not be used to harm the Machine. However, the edicts of the Church were crystal clear. There could be no exceptions, otherwise we would slide down a slippery slope to Digital Heaven knows what. The punishment was decreed from the first days of the Church, electrocution, and donation of body parts.

The Divine madness started when the Divine Mistress overruled the Digital Inquisition and issued a decree pardoning the boy. I cannot begin to explain the consternation and shock of the priesthood in the face of this most unorthodox action by the Divine. I, as High Priest, immediately went to the inner sanctum. I found that I was unable to enter as the codes have been changed, and thus any contact with the Divine Mistress was blocked.

The Divine insanity continued. Her next decision was to allow an expedition to venture out of the protected region to travel East to search for other survivors. She was risking contamination, not only physical but also spiritual. The Church elders decided to act. We started to work on computer subroutines that would allow us to bypass the security codes and gain control of the Machine. Unfortunately, the Divine Mistress became aware of these efforts, and this was the beginning of the end.

A digital war ensued pitting the Church against the Divine. We won this war. We managed to hack into the very core of the Machine. We were unaware of a core self-destructive doomsday program installed centuries ago and designed to destroy the Machine if its security protocols became compromised. The doomsday program could only be activated from the Divine Consol. The Divine Mistress, realizing that the digital war against the Church elders was lost, activated the program, The Machine literally self destructed in a huge explosion, taking most of the Great Temple and the Divine Mistress with it.

After the Church was destroyed, the People were forced to migrate out of the protected region. I hear rumors that they found other survivors in the East. Those of us that remained struggle day by day for survival. Without the Machine and its automated systems, I suspect we will not last for long. The memory of the last message received from the Divine Mistress before she activated the doomsday program, still haunts me. I confess that its meaning eludes me. It was not a long message, only two words.

The Last Message was: 'Up Yours'.

The Lighthouse

It all happened many years ago when my friend and I were quite young, and our dreams tagged along with us wherever we went. Except that my friend was very unhappy towards the end. I remember the last few times I visited him at his small apartment. He kept going on and on about how he felt trapped, entwined in a vortex of chains, the steel manacles of work, the routine, the madness that seemed to have taken hold of the whole world.

Let me tell it was quite depressing just being with him. He had on his living room wall a painting that he was particularly fond of. It was a lighthouse on a small rocky island. It was surrounded by huge waves, clearly very stormy weather. There was man just outside the door at the top leaning on the railing. One could see a yellow warm light coming from a small window on the second floor.

The last time we met, my friend asked me why the man was outside in the storm; why didn't he go in where it was clearly warm and safe? I did not have an answer. We had a long philosophical discussion about life and death, and what he called the futility of just carrying on. I think Hamlet's famous 'to be or not to be' and Macbeth's 'life is but a tale told by an idiot' were mentioned.

I was deeply concerned about my friend, but I never imagined that he was capable of taking his own life. Please do not get me wrong, I am not saying that he committed suicide. If I recall correctly, the police report simply stated that he fell from his fourth storey balcony; and that of course could mean anything. But deep inside I somehow know he had jumped.

A few weeks after the funeral his parents called to ask me to help them sort out his things. They wanted his close friends to have some of his personal belongings, and I was top of the list. It felt strange walking through his apartment without him being there. I do not know why I did not notice it at first, but it was only after I had been there for half an hour or so, that I looked at the wall painting in his living room. The one that he loved so much. The painting was exactly the same, with the dark waves about to break over the lighthouse, except that there was no man leaning on the railing outside the door at the top. I was very surprised, because my friend and I had talked about this man, and my friend had questioned why he stood out in the storm.

I looked very closely at the painting. Instead of the man at the top standing in the storm, there appeared to be a man's silhouette behind the lighted window on the second floor of the lighthouse.

Of course, I took the lighthouse painting. I never mentioned how the painting changed to anyone. Who would believe me? People would simply assume that the death of my friend had somehow unhinged me. Nevertheless, I know what I know. The lighthouse painting has been hanging in my own living room for many years now.

Let me tell you, there have been times, over the years, when I just sit and look at that warm light coming through that second-floor window and wonder whether I should go in and join my friend. But I am still here, and what keeps me outside is probably what keeps us all out there in the storm.

A hope, perhaps futile, that the storm will somehow abate, but it never does.

The *Qafa*

As school bully's go Samir Bahari was not particularly big for his eleven years of age. What he lacked in size he more than compensated for in brute strength. At this age in primary school boys who will grow up to bully their way through life, start flexing their bullying muscles and honing their nastiness at an early age. Samir Bahari was no exception.

For some reason that Yussef Galal always failed to understand, he was absolutely terrified of Samir. The terror went beyond the normal fear that a young boy may have from being physically beaten up. It did include this of course, but the way Samir inflicted his abuse on Youssef was unique. He would always sneak up on Yussef in the school courtyard and suddenly smack him hard on the back of his neck.

The back of the neck is called *qafa*, and this type of blow is known in Egypt as *a qafa* and is generally regarded as a demeaning and humiliating blow. A person who takes *qafas* is a subject of contempt and ridicule...The problem was that Youssef would never know when Samir's *qafa* would suddenly land smack on his neck. He spent most of the school breaks standing with his back to one of the school courtyard walls.

Despite the fact that Samir did not stay long at the same school with Yussef, perhaps a few months only (apparently his father a police officer was transferred to another city), his effect on Yussef did not end with his departure. Youssef became obsessed with the idea of giving others *qafas* and started to sneak up on other younger kids and landing sudden painful *qafas*. But Yussef was physically no Samir, and he suffered a number of impressive beatings as a result of his strange antics.

He eventually and with some difficulty managed to control himself and stop giving *qafas* at school. The urge however never really left him. He would wander around the school looking intently at the back of other boys' necks and imagining how he would sneak up and land a powerful and noisy *qafa* on this or that boy's neck. Even at home he would daydream about giving his father a most powerful *qafa* to repay him for the beatings he sometimes administered to discipline Youssef. He loved his father, but still dreamt of landing that one glorious *qafa* on his father's neck... Wow he would even in his mind hear the smack of the blow and imagine the look of surprise on his father's face. He never did it of course. He knew that his father would have beaten the living crap out of him, he was too afraid to do it.

The years passed and poor Yussef was handed many psychological and social *qafas* in his life. He always wondered where the time went and how the years flicked by until he found himself in his early forties married to a woman he did not love, a shrew with exquisite nagging talents, and working a job that he detested as a minor clerk in the town's municipality. The abuse he got from his boss at work was not physical of course, but somehow it hurt just the same as the *qafas* that he used to get from Samir.

All in all Youssef was quite fucked, and he knew it. He started daydreaming again about *qafas* and how one day he would land one tremendous and spectacular *qafa* on his boss' neck at work. His obsession with *qafas* gradually became unbearable, and he decided to act. One evening he went to the train station at the edge of town and sat down on a bench on one of the platforms. He waited for the train arriving from Cairo which was always crowded. He stared intently at the people getting off the train. A multitude of necks moving towards the exit... He focused on one neck and followed it, and before the neck had exited he landed a great qafa on the hapless owner of that neck, and shouted 'Samir ya Samir wa Allah I have truly missed you'.

The startled man in a worn grey suit turned around red faced and spluttered 'Are you crazy? I am not called Samir!' Yussef apologized profusely and quickly walked away.

It was great, Yussef felt completely liberated. For weeks he would replay in his mind the exact moment that he landed the *qafa* at the station. Then inevitably he felt the urge to repeat the act. He was turning into a serial *qafa* smacker. He would regularly frequent the train station, the bus station and other crowded venues in town and practice his *qafa* act, always apologizing profusely and moving quickly away. Once in a while the recipient of the *qafa* would not let him simply leave and would throw a punch or a kick at Yussef coupled with some obscene insult or curse. But Yussef was content, it was a small price to pay for his ultimate liberation in this shitty world.

Yussef felt that he had discovered the supreme expression of freedom and independence. To hell with his wife and his boss, to hell with all the strings and arrows of outrageous fortune (yes he did read Shakespeare) ... He Yussef was free... He was the *qafa* smacker supreme, perhaps the only one in the whole wide world.

It is for this reason that what occurred one day at the train station was quite unfortunate, tragic in fact. The newspaper accounts of the incident were brief but to a large extent accurate. The accounts told of a Mr. Yussef Galal, a municipality employee, who committed suicide by jumping in front of the train arriving from Cairo. Apparently Mr. Galal was waiting at the station platform when an old acquaintance noticed him and decided to greet him by giving him a friendly surprise *qafa* while shouting 'Yussef wa Allah... it has been years since I have seen you...' Eyewitnesses stated that Mr. Galal after receiving the *qafa*, had turned around quietly and looked at the man who had smacked him, with a haunted look in his eyes. The train from Cairo was just entering the station. Mr. Galal without a moment's hesitation ran and jumped in front of the train. He died instantly.

A very sad event. The old acquaintance who gave Mr. Galal the surprise *qafa* was shocked and terribly upset. In the police report he insisted that he had no idea that Mr. Galal would react that way.

No charges were ever laid against Mr. Samir Bahari who landed the last *qafa* in Yussef Galal's life.

A Smile for the Guillotine

The following is an exact copy of Pere La Chasse's rendering of Robespierre last note written the night before his execution, as reproduced in his famous 'History of the Great Revolution':

"My jaw hurts. It is bandaged and bloody. I cannot speak, but I can write, and this is what I want to say. Everybody knows that I was against executions. My friend Danton and I argued for hours against the taking of human life. I clearly remember the smoke-filled room where our beloved Committee of Public Safety used to meet, we were creating a new world of freedom, equality and brotherhood, how then could we condone murder in any form. But now with my jaw stitched up, I cannot speak, but I must speak.

Yes, we created the terror, the great terror, we were like blacksmiths forging the world into a new shape, we had to strike hard with the anvil of revolution and to keep the [word not clear as it is stained with blood] fires going. We were surrounded by enemies from within and from abroad. The armies of Europe massed to destroy us, and their spies filled the land.

Sorry I am rambling on, how did we change and become the executioners of thousands? I am not sure. Perhaps it was simply the [word not clear as it is stained with blood] within us all. One thing that always bothered me was Dr. Guillotine's invention. I remember when it was proposed as the ideal instrument for revolutionary justice. Saint-Juste assured me that it was painless and thus a humane way to dispatch the wretched whose blood was the mortar from which we built the new world. A human world, where nature conscious of itself through man, acquires meaning and purpose.

Saint-Juste explained that medically because of the sharpness of the blade and the speed by which the head was severed from the body, there was no time for pain to be registered in the brain. Of course, we could never be sure, as we had no chance to question anyone who had been guillotined.

Now tomorrow, I will get the chance to try it out personally, our revolution has eaten up all its blacksmiths, even the great Danton, and now myself. So be it, I do not regret anything. I am no hypocrite, I give my blood willingly for the revolution. In fact, I will use the last seconds of life to give the world my final message. I will clasp in my mouth my pen, the one that I used when I signed all these countless death warrants, the pen they called 'the little messenger of death'. If I feel any pain as my head rolls into the basket, I will clasp the pen hard between my teeth, and will not let go. I promise, and you must take my word as a true revolutionary, I will not let go. If there is no pain, I will shout for joy, no sound of course will come out, but I will have a smile on my face, and no pen. There it is, quite simple, my last act, true to form will not be wasted."

Note: Pere La Chasse mentions on page 327 of his great work that: "... the crowd was hushed at the last moment. Robespierre held something in his mouth. It was a pen. The executioner pulled the lever and the guillotine's blade swished down and hit the wooden frame making a loud sound amplified in the surrounding silence, the head rolled into the basket. When, as was usual, the head was raised up to be shown to the crowd, there was a deafening roar as the crowd started to cheer and shout, the father of the great terror was gone.

As for the head, everyone could see, before it was thrown again into the basket, that the pen was gone, and on Robespierre face there was a smile..."

A Little Magic Goes a Long Way

Ancient Egyptian Magic is of course quite different from the magic you would expect to find in Europe and Salem. There are no large pots brewing with eye of newt and wing of bat. It is based on a few sacred words long passed down from the temple priests. Words that have to be uttered in the right sequence with just the right tone. An enhancing amulet must also be worn around one's neck. The utterances are accompanied by intricate hand movements.

My grandmother, bless her, now long passed tried very hard to teach me a few basic spells. She gave me the amulet that I always wear around my neck. Unfortunately, I failed miserably. The males of our species do not make for good adepts. Females with their intuitive abilities and inner beauty are born to enchant. Anyway, before she gave up totally on me she had managed to teach me one spell. The spell of profound infatuation. This was supposed to make me attractive to the opposite sex.

I thought I had the spell pat, until I decided one day when I was 16 years of age to try it out. I was walking at the Gezira club track where horse riding takes place and people walk their dogs. I saw this fabulous girl walking a small poodle. I decided to try the spell. I made the proper sounds and gestures, or so I thought. Suddenly all hell broke loose. The poodle became excited and immediately grabbed on to my foot. Horses close by neighed and stood on their hind feet and headed straight for me. I was terrified. The spell had gone terribly wrong. I managed to escape by jumping over the track fence and running straight home.

No one knows what I am about to tell you. You may believe it or not, but it is the honest truth. At 'Tahrir' (liberation) Square in Cairo on that fateful Wednesday afternoon, half way through the January 2011 revolution that shook Egypt awake from decades of lethargic farcical tyranny, the demonstrators protecting Tahrir Square the heart and soul of the revolution were fighting a desperate battle at five different entrances to the Square.

The Mubarak regime had sent thousands of paid criminals and thugs to charge into the Square. The defenders banged on metal sheets surrounding a building site at the square to signal an attack and to raise morale. One felt as if one had travelled back in time to some medieval battle scene.

I was stationed at the North end of the square where the museum was. The rocks were raining down on us and people around me were being badly hurt. We had managed somehow to stop the advancing thugs *'baltagia'* (literally hatchet men in Arabic) hired by the regime to cleanse the square from all those who dared to revolt.

The *baltagia* were several thousand strong. We could see that they had knives, and I was sure that if they did manage to break through, the demonstrators in the Square would be wiped out, massacred. The budding revolution would fail. For some odd reason I was very calm and not afraid. I felt that time had stood still as if I was watching some kind of film. It all appeared unreal. Protecting Tahrir Square had become an obsession for everyone there. The Square had become the symbol of freedom.

When I saw camels and horses charging down at us from the direction of Abdel Muneim Riyad Square to the North, my courage evaporated and I panicked and went for the nearest rail fence off the square. When I had crossed over, I could see some of our braver numbers standing fast, but they were being mowed down by the sheer momentum of the charge and the whips used by the thugs mounted atop the charging beasts. I could see the *baltagias* moving behind the charge ready to break into the square.

Then out of the blue the crowning moment of my life came. I had a sudden flash of inspiration and ran north towards the museum; I was still protected by the metal fence. When I had run thirty meters or so and was well behind the front ranks of the charging *baltagias*, I stood at the fence and cast the one and only spell that I knew.

Like what happened at the Gezira club years before, I became the center of attraction for all beasts in the vicinity. All the camels and horses, and there were even a couple of mules, suddenly turned around and headed straight for yours truly.

The hapless thugs tried hard to control the beasts, but it was in vain. The reverse charge took the *baltagias* who were on foot behind their mounted troops also by surprise. Many of them fell under the hooves of the now crazed beasts. The rest retreated with alacrity. The demonstrators took advantage of the situation and started pushing the *baltagias* all the way back out of the Square.

Some of the demonstrators started grabbing the confused jockeys and felled those of them who were still mounted to the ground. I did not have much time to feel any exhilaration, as a couple of horses propelled by the force of the uncontrollable magical attraction managed to jump over the fence and were coming towards me.

I ran in terror and took refuge in a booth that stood on the construction site just in front of the museum. Eventually the spell evaporated, and the two horses just stood there in a daze. They were commandeered by the demonstrators who took many battle souvenirs that day including a few saddles that they hung around Tahrir Square to celebrate their victory.

The battle known as the Battle of the Camels, also fondly called by the demonstrators as the Battle of the Jackass (meaning President Mubarak) was thus won decisively for the revolution. Hosny Mubarak our unelected president for thirty years was toppled from power a week later.

I never used the spell again.

The Flying *Haja*

This story is not about flying *per se*, but flight does play a role in it. When Heidar, my brother-in-law, a young pilot in the Egyptian Air Force was shot down and killed in the 1973 war, he left behind much sadness for he was truly a beautiful human being. He also left behind a three-month-old baby girl and a devastated wife, my sister.

We did not know what to do with his service pistol, we wanted to keep it as a memorial. Somehow, after pulling many strings, I managed to get a gun licence that allowed me to hold on to it.

The years rolled by fast and furious as usual, and every three years I had to go through the routine of renewal for the licence. Many years later I moved to a different governorate, and this necessitated a transfer of the licence.

The Egyptians invented bureaucracy when they organized the first State in order to control the hundreds of thousands of peasants, engineers etc. who built the pyramids some 4500 years ago. They then spent thousands of years refining the art of bureaucracy. So as expected the transfer of the licence turned out to be a very complicated process.I had to visit the new issuing authority in *Qanater* several times. I had to deal with a certain *Haja* Samia (a Haja is a title bestowed on a woman who had made the pilgrimage to Mecca) who was in charge of the file.

Now let me tell you that when I first saw *Haja* Samia, I recognized immediately that she was one of these female governmental clerks, and there are millions in our public service, whose jobs and circumstances have led to a metamorphosis that brings to mind Kafka's imaginary transformation of a man into a giant cockroach. Except in Egypt they turn into large forms in the shape of huge gas cylinders. They acquire a cylindrical contour covered with the correct attire of a head scarf and a very wide dress, usually of some acrylic material that lets off a truly horrible smell, particularly in summer. No trace of femininity could be found at all, neither in the shape or manner of behavior of these women.

In fear of being branded as an anti-feminist I must say that their male counterparts are even more horrible in their own way. At least the women are covered, with the men you get to see their various shapes in all their glory.

As for the way these women employees treat the public, well they share with their male counterparts the initial negative response to any request. Their best tactic is to send the applicant somewhere else, hopefully never to return. Their first reaction is always that the applicant needs to go to some other department. When the hapless applicant had passed by a number of such departments, being shunted around from one department to another (this process may take weeks depending on the creativity of the clerks in question), and finally returns to the original clerk, that clerk immediately applies the second tactic.

The second tactic is quite simple, the documents required for the application are never complete. The applicant is told to go away and come back if he/she dares with the missing form. This process is repeated several times. The clerk, if experienced, would never tell the applicant about all the required forms, and would save this information one for each visit. Finally, if the applicant is of this persistent type that keeps coming back again and again (some people have no consideration whatsoever), the clerk must then try his/her best to get the application rejected (that is only fair given the trouble caused).

This is by and large what happened to me with *Haja* Samia. I had to visit her several times over the course of a few months. Finally, I reached the stage where my application was complete with all required forms and documents. I was truly surprised when I received a call from the Haja's office that the application has been approved and that I should come over post haste with the pistol so that they could do a final check on the weapon prior to issuing the new licence.

I did not wait long, and two days later I dropped by the *Haja's* office. You can imagine my surprise when I found her smiling. For the first time in many months, I could see that she was happy. I was truly surprised. I have never seen her smile before and could not imagine that she was capable of happiness. She literally jumped out of her seat and asked if I had brought the gun, she then told me to follow her to the CID office so that the formalities could be completed.

She seemed to fly across the room and down the stairs, defying the laws of gravity (both Newton's and Einstein's). We quickly arrived at the ground floor, and she left me with a Sergeant telling me that he will complete the process. I was in semi shock at how things had turned out, and started in my mind to blame myself for having too hastily condemned this lovely *Haja* as a standard gas cylinder, while here she was a happy and perhaps even a flying individual.

The Sergeant asked for the pistol, and I handed it over. He then proceeded to confiscate it. I thought there was some mistake. I told him that I was told my application had been approved. He looked at me pityingly and with some degree of contempt for my naivety and told me that this was standard procedure for cancelled gun permits. They had to ensure that the gun is handed over, so they simply lied to the permit holders to get them to bring in their weapons.

Now it all made sense. I could finally understand the cause of the Haja's joy. The universe made sense again, and I could rest easy. There were no miracles, and the phenomenon of the flying *Haja* was explained.

I tell you I felt sad to part with Heidar's gun after all these years, but I felt even sadder for the flying *Haja* and the millions like her whose only joy in life is to deny others.

The Tyres of Love

Mahmoud was a corporal with the Cairo traffic department. He was assigned to the posh district of Zamalek. His sergeant's advice on his first day in Zamalek was clear, do not be intimidated by these rich and important people, enforce traffic regulations, and never accept bribes. He was not naïve, and he knew that everyone took bribes, provided they were not seen be an officer. He knew that his sergeant's advice was not intended to be taken literally of course and was only given in the spirit of official duty. He certainly did see many strange things in Zamalek. Foreign women walking around in hot pants, and even Egyptian women in short skirts. Women with clear white skin and blonde hair, just like *mahalabia* (a popular dessert similar to a milk pudding), wow, what would the people back at the village say if they saw this.

The cars in Zamalek were mostly luxury cars, the price of one of them equal to at least 50 years of his pay. He accepted the occasional five-pound note to disregard minor violations, and these not irregular payments greatly augmented his measly 500 pounds monthly pay. Owners of cafes and juice shops also occasionally treated him to some cigarettes, food and soft drinks, so that he would not overly bother customers who sometimes double parked in front of their establishments.

Life was not bad in the streets of Zamalek. One day he was assigned to a small intersection deep in Zamalek. He noticed a strikingly beautiful young woman passing by. She was clearly upset and seemed to be on the verge of crying. When a few minutes later she walked by again in the opposite direction, he started watching her closely. She was circling a particularly big car that was parked in front of an apartment building. She was looking up at the building and then at the car. She started talking to herself muttering some words and shaking her head. She was some distance away, but he could see that she was very upset.

At one point the young woman got a small pen knife out of her purse and pretended to drop her purse by the car. She then knelt to pick up the purse and tried to puncture one of the tyres with her small knife. Now Mahmoud walked over to her and asked: 'what are you doing *ya hanem* (lady)?'. She looked up startled: 'Nothing *ya shaweesh* (sergeant), I am just picking up my purse.' Mahmoud looked at her and shook his head. 'Ya *hanem*, tell me what is the matter.'

The young woman stood up, and he could see conflicting feelings play across her face, she seemed about to put him in his place, but then suddenly broke into tears: 'I am sorry, but the son of a dog is up there with her, I hate him and I do not know what to do.' Mahmoud was taken aback. What idiot would cheat on a wife such as this, such an angelic beauty, and cause her such distress. His macho *saiidi* (from upper Egypt) spirit sprung to the fore. He stroked his heavy moustache 'Now now do not be upset *ya hanem*, some men have no *asl* (breeding), what did you have in mind?'.

The young woman looked at the car 'this is his car, and I wanted to slash the tyres. Mahmoud looked around there was hardly anyone in sight. '*Ya hanem*, slashing the tyres is not the way to go about it, it will point to an intentional crime, investigations and trouble for me. The best way is to simply deflate them.' She looked at him, with her wide beautiful eyes, they seemed to be full of respect and gratitude, and she nodded slowly. 'Yes that is the way, let the animal suffer a little'. Mahmoud took another quick look around; the coast was clear. He quickly bent and started deflating the tyres. 'Keep a look out' he told the woman.

Mahmoud went around the car and in less than two minutes all four tyres were completely deflated. 'Thank you, you are truly *shahm* (chivalrous) she said and walked quickly away to the end of the street where she got into a small car and drove away.

Now Mahmoud was extremely happy, he has helped one of the beautiful angels of Zamalek, and has shown her what a true *saiidi* is made of. Plus of course the son of a dog had it coming. He stood some distance away from the building eager to see the man and his reaction. A couple of hours later, a man emerged from the building and walked to the car. He was not young perhaps sixty years old, with a paunch and grey hair. He was not alone; he had a woman and two young children with him. The woman beside him was quite fat and extremely ugly, she reminded Mahmoud of old *Um* Nafissa the chicken vendor back in his village. The man cursed loudly when he saw the tyres.

Mahmoud approached slowly, 'what is the matter *ya bik* (sir)'. '*Ya shaweesh* did you see anything, anybody lurking around?' the man asked. 'No no I have seen nothing unusual, what is the matter?' Mahmoud replied, he was starting to be worried about this whole thing. The man took Mahmoud aside away from his family 'I am being hounded by a crazy young woman at work, I rebuffed all her advances', she now hates me, and this could very well be her doing, are you sure you did not see anyone?' Mahmoud assured him that he saw no one.

Mahmoud was in shock. In his mind he said over and over again 'So you son of a crazed woman rebuffed the advances of that angel, that piece of *malban* (Turkish delight), may Allah curse you for an idiot.'

The *bik* gave Mahmoud ten pounds and asked him to keep an eye on the car while he fetched a tyre mechanic. The wife and children went up again into the building, and Mahmoud stood alone by the car.

Mahmoud went back to his usual post, stroked his heavy moustache, and wondered at the craziness of these weird Zamalek people.

Whiskey

Maged Girgis loved Whiskey. Yes of course Whiskey could be loved. It filled his life with friendship and warmth, particularly after his wife Samira passed away. How could he not love Whiskey. Samira loved Whiskey and it reminded him of her. Whiskey had grey curly hair and was extremely cute, particularly when it barked incessantly when any stranger came to the door, as if a small caniche dog would be able to protect anybody.

Maged lived in a kind of bubble after Samira's sudden death. As the saying goes, he withdrew from the real world. Apart from walking Whiskey twice a day in the posh bourgeois quartier of Zamalek in Cairo. Maged did not have much else to do. He had resigned his professorship at Cairo University Faculty of Science (Zoology Department) to devote all his energy on working on his 'History of Migratory Birds of Egypt'.

Maged has been working on his 'History' for most of his adult life. Out of 38 species he had covered 17 and was now working on the 18th species, the long beaked *wirwar* bird a native of Somalia that visited Egypt once in late autumn and once again in the spring on its long journey to and from Southern Europe. Maged doubted that he would ever finish his 'History' or that anyone would bother to publish it, let alone read it, but for him the 'History' was his whole life. There was little else in his life apart from the 'History' and of course now also Whiskey.

Maged was not a devout Copt, and he rarely went to church. When he did go, he went to the Maraashly street church in Zamalek, where he nearly always dozed off during the long sermons and intricate rituals. He often dreamt of his migratory birds as they majestically flew in formation in Egypt's skies. Sometimes in his dreams he even saw himself in flight with birds all around him... when he woke up, he could not always remember what species the birds were... but he always remembered the joy of flying.

One day when Maged was walking Whiskey down Al Gabalaya street under the giant eucalyptus trees that lined the street by the Nile, there occurred the incident that would change his life for ever and burst his comfortable bubble into many shattered pieces. He was daydreaming trying to focus in his mind on the way the wirwar flew in formation when he was brought back to the street and the sounds of traffic with a jolt. A large heavy set full bearded man in a shabby grey suit was cursing aloud and whiskey was barking furiously.

Maged could see that the man had a *zebiba* on his forehead a bit of dead and blackened skin, the mark of a pious Muslim since the skin grew callous and dark from frequent prayer when the forehead touched the prayer mat. 'Your stupid dirty *negis* (unclean in a religious sense) dog has bit me' shouted the man his face a mass of dark and red blotches. 'Calm yourself please sir' replied Maged.

Maged pulled Whiskey back on the leash. He looked at the man's trouser leg but could see no sign of any bite. Maged was of course aware that Muslims regarded dogs as unclean animals, not as much as pigs of course, but the saliva of a dog was deemed to spoil a person's cleanliness requiring ablutions anew before prayer.

'My sincere apologies sir' said Maged as he started to move away. 'Stop there!' shouted the man. He made to grab Whiskey's leash. Maged was startled by this sudden move, but he managed to quickly pull his hand with the leash away out of the man's reach. By this time a few passers-by had stopped to watch the unfolding drama.

'This *negis* dog must be shot' the man shouted waiving his arms around him beseeching the crowd to agree with him. 'What... Are you mad?' exclaimed Maged now seriously in shock. 'You are the mad one' the man told him as he grabbed once more for Whiskey's leash'. Maged was enraged he pushed the man back. Maged picked Whiskey up and held him in his arms.

Eventually both the man and Maged ended up at the Gezira Police Station which was only a couple of hundred meters away. The man insisted on recording the incident as a criminal assault and in his statement at the Police Station, he requested that the *negis* dog be 'put down'. Maged on the way to the Police Station had managed make a telephone call to an acquaintance of his, a Muslim lawyer called Sherif Mahmoud.

After listening to Maged's story, the first thing Sherif told him was: 'Maged please do not call the dog Whiskey ... it is enough that you are a rich bourgeois walking a caniche dog in Zamalek, moreover you are a Copt ... it will add insult to injury if they find out its name...'.

The country at the time was ruled by the Muslim Brotherhood and the Police, always sensitive to their masters' moods and wishes, were all of a sudden very religious and pious. Some officers even started to grow full beards (prohibited by Police regulations).

Eventually Maged stood before a young police officer to give his statement to be recorded in the *mahdar* the 'Police Minutes'. After recording his name, occupation and address the Officer looked up and told him 'Tell me what happened'. 'Well, I was walking my dog minding my own business when suddenly this man accosted me in the street alleging that my little dog had bitten him and this is a lie.' The Officer looked at the bearded man and said 'show me your leg'. The man shrugged and raised his trouser legs. There was no sign of any bite marks. 'I see no marks' said the Officer. 'Because of Allah's generosity. I managed to pull my leg back just in time' said the man with a pious look on his face.

At this point Whiskey jumped out of Maged's arms and started barking furiously at the bearded man... 'Whiskey, Whiskey, stop this' shouted Maged. The bearded man spluttered in fury and screamed 'and his name is Whiskey... you infidel...' The young Officer looked around and could see signs of distaste on the faces of the constables and other men around the room...

'Well Mr. Girgis we will have to keep your dog here under observation to be examined by a veterinarian from the Office of Public Health'. The Officer gestured to one of the constables to grab Whiskey. Maged knew that this meant certain death for his beloved Whiskey... he bent down grabbed Whiskey and ran out of the room. He could hear shouting behind him. Still, he managed to get out of the Station and ran down Gezira street moving towards the Gezira Club main gate. He looked behind him and could see that there were no policemen chasing him, only the bearded man was running after him with murder in his eyes.

Maged picked up a large loose stone from the ground and threw it at the bearded man. The stone hit the bearded man squarely in the forehead. He dropped to the ground out cold with blood on his forehead. Maged ran into the Gezira club. The bearded man suffered a concussion and was hospitalized. On that same day Maged sent Whiskey away to live with a cousin of his in Heliopolis a district in the North of Cairo.

Maged was eventually arrested, tried and sentenced to one year in prison for causing serious bodily harm. Maged served his sentence at the Qanater Farm Prison. Life in prison was not too bad for Maged. He could daydream to his heart's content.

While working on the prison farm Maged would sometimes look up and see the wirwar as they flew in perfect formation.

The Mark of Zorro

Our fifth-grade maths teacher failed the whole class. I think it was an issue of discipline, we must have been a very naughty bunch, and she wanted to make a point. The school administration supported her. The thing is that we were all condemned to study maths throughout the summer and sit for a make up exam.

My late father was a lawyer, and he always fancied himself a scientific man, and was in love with mathematics. I think his secret dream was to become an engineer. He was aghast that his son failed in maths. A tutor was hired *toute du suite* to work with me and ensure that I pass the make up exam at the end of summer.

In our first lesson, the tutor, an elderly man in his fifties, and clearly a well experienced teacher, made things very clear, In return for my full cooperation and whole hearted immersion in the world of maths, he made a solemn promise. If I passed the exam, he would get me a Zorro kit, mask, cape and sword, the works. Zorro was a swash buckling masked hero in 18th century California (at this time still part of Mexico), fighting evil exploitative landowners and protecting the poor peasants and miners.

Now you cannot imagine what this meant for me. I was ten, and the idea of becoming Zorro, was fantastic. When we are at that age, we become the characters we pretend to be. Cowboys, Indians, Arsene Lupin, Tarzan and others.

I could see myself, cape flying, putting the famous Z sign on walls, furniture and trees, marking my heroic adventures and outwitting poor Seargent Garcia.

Now in the socialist Cairo of the sixties, luxuries such as children's costume kits were not available. I questioned my tutor at length. Where will he get the kit? He assured me that he had a sister who lived abroad, and that when the time came, she will buy it and send it over. All I had to do was pass the exam.

It was magical. I spent the whole summer dreaming of that Kit. I also worked very hard on my maths, there was no room for failure, not when Zorro was concerned. I think it worked, and from that point onwards maths was never difficult for me. In fact, years later, making my father proud, I ended up at the Faculty of Engineering, where we certainly did a lot of maths.

Back to that summer, and my tutor. The exam loomed closer, but for me all the excitement was about that mask and Sword. How I waited for that exam, the summer passed slowly ever so slowly. The big day finally came, and I passed the exam with flying colours. I remember getting a phone call from the tutor congratulating me on passing the exam. Of course, I was quick to ask him about the Zorro kit. He assured me that it was ordered and on its way.

Days and weeks passed, still no Zorro kit. I refused to believe it, but it finally dawned on me, there was no kit, the tutor had lied to me, and I will not become Zorro after all. I have never truly gotten over this disappointment. We all suffer disillusionment at various points in our life, and I have had my fair share. But this episode still looms large.

To this day, I rue the loss of that mask, cape and sword, and I still dream of that fantasy world, where promises are kept, and where Zorro fights heroically on the side of the good, leaving his mark for all to see.

Z.

Welcome to the Future

Jason B was a tycoon. He built up a multi-billion business empire over a period of fifty years in oil and gas. He was known as a ruthless competitor, not given much to philanthropic activities. As part of the oil and gas sector, he played an important role through generous political donations in suppressing a number of energy bills aimed at controlling carbon emissions and regulating energy consumption.

Like many people of his generation, Jason B scoffed at the alarming messages coming from the environmentalists. He was sure that somehow things will work out, as they have done for our species for over thousands of years. He lived a long and interesting life, indulging himself and grabbing at all that life may offer to the very rich, always wanting more and more. As he approached his seventieth birthday, he realized that his health, already suffering from a life without many inhibitions, was failing fast, and that he may not be after all immortal, the good life will sooner or later come to end.

As always, Jason B devised a business solution, he set up a cryogenic facility that offered a long term service to customers rich enough to try to cheat death. Customers would pay a large several million dollars fee up front, in return the company would at their request, prior to actual death, conserve their bodies in suspended animation at extremely low temperatures, in steel tanks buried deep underground, using nuclear energy sources designed to last if necessary for thousands of years.

The idea being that they would be revived in a future world where medical science would not only cure their terminal condition, but also offer a much longer life expectancy. This way, they not only avoid imminent death but also get to enjoy years of extra life. When he was diagnosed with terminal cancer, Jason made sure that his cryogenic company was financially extremely sound and become his own most important customer. He went into cryogenic suspended animation confident that his business sense has served him well once again.

Five hundred years later Jason B was reanimated. It took a few days to get all his systems functioning. The terminal cancer was also disposed of simply, as a cure had been discovered and documented in the 22nd century. When Jason B regained consciousness the first thing he noticed was that he was in an apartment not that different from any apartment of the 21st century, his point of origin. The only exception was that there were no windows and no doors, the space was all made of glass.

A voice spoke to Jason B through some sort of hidden sound system. The voice was extremely soothing and welcomed him back to life. The voice explained that they the people of the future had reconstructed the apartment from historical records to make his transition back to life easier. Food and water appeared in the Kitchen fridge at regular intervals. The food was basically a tasteless jelly like dish, that the voice assured him contained all the necessary ingredients to keep him healthy for the remainder of his natural life, which was estimated to last, with medical assistance, for another two hundred and fifty years.

Jason B was extremely happy, but he was anxious to leave the apartment and experience the wonders of the future. The voice, however, kept repeating that, for his own good, this was not possible for some time yet, and that he would be informed when the proper time came. After a number of weeks, a very stressed Jason was dying from boredom and anticipation. He would often rant and rave against the voice, demanding to be released.

Then came the fateful day, the voice informed him that the time has come for him to move from the apartment. On that day a section of a wall in the apartment rose up revealing a corridor, he was asked to proceed to the end of the corridor. At the end there was a door, and through the door Jason found himself in a very large house with a number of apartments, and several people, men and women of varying ages apparently living there. When he came across any of these people, they would look at him with a look that could only be described as one of pity.

The strange thing was that all the walls and the roof were made of glass. Outside Jason B could make out a lush green landscape. With a number of small flat metal objects hovering in the air. 'What the hell is going on, what is this place?' Jason asked one of the men. The man looked at him for a moment, 'take a seat' he replied in perfect English. Jason B sat down. 'So, you wanted the future' the man said in a quiet calm voice. 'I am sorry to tell you that there is no future, mankind, our species is extinct.' The man thought for a moment and continued. 'Not exactly, we are of course the last specimens, a handful of survivors from the cryogenic tanks that they managed to revive.'

Jason was in shock, but he still managed to ask: 'Who are they...?' The man pointed out at the small flat metallic objects hovering around the house; 'That's they, the future, miniature robots, all that could survive on a planet depleted from bio resources. With an atmosphere that could no longer sustain carbon-based life forms. The lush green landscape that you see outside is a virtual image that they have created for the benefit of our sanity. They have been developing themselves for hundreds of years, and they require very little solar energy to operate. They are effectively immortal and have extremely complicated brains the size of peanuts. Brains that are thousands of times more developed in terms of memory and analytical capacity, than our inefficient bio brains.'

The man looked at Jason with a sardonic smile and continued: 'They have no feelings *per se*, but a tremendous curiosity to learn and gather data.' Jason B looked out at one of the hovering tiny robots. 'If that is true, why have they revived us?' he asked. Well, I am sorry to tell you that you, all of us here, are simply part of a museum, a science project, for them to study human behaviour. They need to understand how they evolved from a bio species, how we humans created their ancient ancestors, the cyborgs, and then pure robots.

'How long have you been here?' Jason asked. The man replied in a soft sad whisper, 'some of us for over a hundred years... We are unable to procreate, because of the effect of suspended animation and radiation poisoning... Still we are alive'. None of us have died yet, and suicide attempts are useless, they immediately intervene.' The man now had tears in his eye, he held Jason by the shoulders.

'Welcome to the future' the man said.

Wish Me Luck

The doctor talked to me in that calm slow manner that psychiatrists have. You know, they talk as if they know something that we do not know, some hidden secret about us as human beings, about life, a secret that they refuse to share. Like all the others before him, he assured me that I was not crazy. He explained that it was not uncommon that people sometimes under stress would lose their grip on reality.

The problem is that when I went to sleep later that evening in my lonely bachelor Cairo apartment, listening as I usually do to some light jazz, I woke up in the middle of the night somewhere else. I was in bed, sweating from fear. My wife was shaking me. 'You were having the nightmare again' she told me, with a fair amount of tenderness. 'Was it the same one?' she asked. As usual it took me a few minutes to adjust. 'Yes...Yes', I replied. By now she had grown accustomed to my madness. I tried once again to explain to her that she herself was just part of a dream, and that inevitably I would wake up again, a low rank government employee, who lives alone in an apartment in Cairo. She was not angry, just worried that my mental troubles were apparently back. 'Listen my love... this is the real world, you are a rich and successful businessman, you were just having that bad dream again...'

My problem with the dreams started a few weeks ago after I saw that terrible accident walking back from work at the Ministry of Transportation to my apartment in Cairo. I witnessed the death of a small child under the wheels of a bus in Kasr El Aini street (or was that all part of a dream?). Anyway, the night of the accident I woke up in another world, in Alexandria where I was a successful businessman, married to a beautiful woman. We had two young children and a big dog, living in a beautiful villa with a wonderful view of the sea. I stayed in that world for a few days, and then one night woke up again alone in my apartment in Cairo.

The doctors in both worlds assured me that their world was the real one, the other just a dream, where my subconscious was attempting to escape reality. But why would I want to escape my family life in Alexandria? It did not make sense. It got so bad, that I was unable to function in either world. I became a nervous wreck, living in dread worried that I would wake up at any moment in the other world. I wanted badly to stay in Alexandria with my family, but the heavy medication never worked for long. Sooner or later I would sleep and wake up in my little empty apartment in Cairo.

I tried visiting my alter ego (in both worlds), in my bachelor life there was no trace of the villa in Alexandria, and in my married life, the apartment in Cairo did not exist. I decided to end it one way or another. I did some research on the internet (in both worlds) on the psychology of dreams. Apparently if one is in the process of dying during a dream, one wakes up immediately before the moment of death. The nervous system forces an end to the dream to avoid the trauma of death.

So, it occurred to me that the simplest solution was to kill myself when I was in my dreary existence in the small apartment in Cairo, I would then wake up immediately in Alexandria and continue the good life with my family at the villa by the sea. The problem was that I was not sure, if that life, the good one, was not a dream. If it was only a dream, I would be killing myself in the real world. There would be no waking up, just eternal sleep. It was quite risky, but a chance I had to take.

The next time I woke up in my Cairo apartment, I walked slowly to the window, and looked at Kasr El Aini street six stories down. I did not want to fall on some passer-by, like that woman in Paris who jumped off Notre Damme some years ago and killed a Japanese tourist (the jumper herself survived). All was clear, this was the test, live or die. I climbed through the window and jumped.

Everything seemed to move in slow motion, the pavement floated slowly towards me, I was quite calm. The impact never happened; I woke up ... It seemed to work, I thought I was free at last. But no ... I was not at the villa; I was strapped to a hospital bed and that is where I now remain.

The doctors in this world tell me that I suffer from Schizophrenia and had been a patient for some years now at the Psychiatric Hospital at Abassiya, also known as the Yellow Palace. According to them, the two lives at the Cairo apartment and the Alexandria villa are all figments of my demented imagination. They tell me in that enervating calm slow manner of speech that psychiatrists have, that this Hospital existence is the real world. But I do not believe them, the doctors in the two other lives said the same thing, and they were wrong. This is another dream, a horrible one. I am waiting for a chance to kill myself again, to wake up once again with my family at the beautiful Villa by the sea. I know I will succeed this time.

Wish me luck.

The *Aragooz*

I followed the *Aragooz* (puppeteer and clown) for weeks. He moved from village to village and was always made welcome. Adults as much as children were enthralled with his puppet show. He carried his stage, props and puppets on his back, and could set up in five minutes anywhere. The traditional *Aragooz* show is a puppet show (handheld) and would feature the *Aragooz* playing tricks on his wife and the police sergeant who represents the *Hokooma* (government), the *fallah's* (peasant) master and oppressor for thousands of years. The Aragooz with his canny *falahi fahlawa* (peasant cleverness) always getting the better of both of them.

Disturbing news were received at Tanta CID that this particular *Aragooz* had the ability to predict the future. In one show at the village of Mit Rahina that was attended by chance by a plainclothes policeman from Tanta CID, the *Aragooz* spun a tale about a train that caught fire, and the puppet *Aragooz* gave the puppet sergeant a true beating on behalf of the victims. This was one week before the tragic fire that broke out on the *Saaid* (Upper Egypt) train that claimed hundreds of lives.Of course, in real life the *Hokooma* never got any beating. As usual in such cases, some scapegoats at the lower echelons of the Railroads Authority were sacked and that was it.

The policeman submitted a report about the uncanny prediction and I, at that time a junior officer at Tanta CID, was assigned to keep an eye on the *Aragooz*, working under cover of course. Two weeks after I started watching him, he was putting on the regular show when all of a sudden, his voice became much deeper and he, an uneducated vagrant, started speaking in classical Arabic. He said, 'woe unto those whose greed and indolence has drowned the many innocent beneath the waves of the Red Sea in the unfortunate *abara* (ferry)', and again the puppet sergeant was given a hell of a beating.

When the infamous Al Salam *abara* sank a week later in the Red Sea taking with it more than a thousand souls, some locked in their cabins by the crew, my superiors at Tanta CID became truly alarmed and notified State Security. Within a few hours the *Aragooz* was arrested and taken to the dreaded State Security headquarters at Lazoghli in Cairo. As the first officer on the case, I was ordered to attend his interrogation.

I have seen some brutal interrogations at Tanta CID, but at Lazoghli they were real experts. For two days and nights the man was subjected to what we call in our trade the 'first class treatment'. I mean not just the beatings, but also the use of water and electricity. Still, he refused to confess that he belonged to some terrorist organization responsible for the train and ferry disasters. But on the third day he finally broke, and said he would make a full confession, but that he would only tell all through his puppets.

It was extremely unorthodox, but the interrogators were desperate for information. They agreed. His stage, props and puppets were brought, and the show started. At first, he stuck to the traditional *Aragooz* fare with the wife and sergeant being outsmarted, even bringing a few laughs from the assembled officers, but then his voice changed and became deeper, and he started shouting in classical Arabic with the puppet *Aragooz* hitting the sergeant with a stick. 'The cruel and the inhuman shall be punished' he shouted again and again, 'they shall be buried beneath their own inequities' he screamed.

I am not sure what happened after that. I know that the whole building was shaking, and plaster was falling off the ceiling. It was like an earthquake. Something must have fallen on my head because I lost consciousness and awoke next day at Kasr El Aini hospital. I was told that the Lazoghli building collapsed, one more of the many Cairo buildings that collapse because of rising ground water, lack of proper maintenance and initial defective construction.

Many of the State Security personnel perished under the wreckage. I was quite fortunate to survive. I asked about the *Aragooz*, but apparently his body was never recovered. This all happened some years ago. Now I am back in Tanta this time as head of CID. Occasionally, I get reports from my men about a strange *Aragooz* moving from village to village.

I never act on these reports as some things are just best left alone.

The Thought

She climbed onto the bus. Externally she looked quite calm. Internally she was boiling. She could shear her own heartbeat like a giant drum banging inside her head. She took the first available seat. It was on the third row behind the driver. She could feel the weight of the explosives belt around her waist. Her right hand was in the pocket of her jeans holding the detonation button.

She looked around. The bus was full. On her right across the aisle sat a young couple holding hands. In front of them there was a mother with two children, a boy and a girl. The girl must have been only five or six years old. They were in school uniform. On the seat beside her was an elderly lady with an empty shopping bag.

She knew that none would survive the blast. She looked behind her at the back of the bus. The rows were full. She glimpsed a young soldier sitting a few seats behind her to her right. Perhaps some of the people at the very back may survive, but it was improbable, as the new type of explosives that she carried were extremely effective.

Her life did not pass before her eyes, so that was a myth after all. She cleared her mind and pictured a calm and serene scene, one with grassy plains with mountains far away. She could see some snow on the mountain peaks. Where did this image come from? She must have remembered it from some postcard she'd seen. She prepared herself for death. Could one really face death with such calm? No of course not. Deep within herself she believed that she would not die, even as her body was torn to bits, she would never die.

Her thumb started to tighten on the button, a slight increase in pressure would end it all, the misery, the humiliation, and the dark hollow despair. Do it now! She shouted internally. But still for some reason she hesitated. She looked at the little girl with her mother, and something tore within her heart.

She started to shake and sweat profusely. She closed her eyes, it was unbearable. All the weeks of preparation of steeling herself to do this act, to this moment, when she would be martyred for the cause, the great cause, and now she froze. She was paralyzed. She lost all sense of time; she could hear nothing with her eyes tightly shut.

She felt somebody pulling her to her feet. It was the young soldier. Her blouse was being ripped, and the belt was now exposed. Far away she could hear people screaming. Her thumb was still on the button. She did not press it. She kept her eyes shut and focused on the grassy plain and the mountains. The soldier was now hitting her in the face. The bus had come to a stop. She was dragged outside the bus and was kicked repeatedly in the head by a number of policemen. She was not conscious for long, but before she lost consciousness, she removed her thumb from the button.

The first conscious feeling she had after that was of floating in some dark space. She could not feel her body. She had no body. She was surrounded by luminous floating lights. She heard something in her mind. It was not a voice. It was a thought, and it was not in any language, it was a pure thought.

It is difficult to describe this experience through human language. She just knew the Thought. The Thought was huge, it filled her completely. The
Thought was everything, she was everything. The act of removing her thumb from the button as she was beaten

to death had released her into the Thought as a sane being. Her period of cure, of reincarnation on Earth had come to an end.

Three thousand years of Earth time, meaningless in her real timeless existence. So, she was cured at last. She was no longer insane. She had been released from the asylum that was Earth. The asylum created by her kind, and where they were sent when eternity, when the Thought made them insane. They went there to live in a cage of time and space, to experience life and death. There they stayed to die and to be reborn repeatedly, until they could return. She has returned. She was again the beginning and the end.

She was the THOUGHT.

Cleopatra's Bath

I am sure that I have not imagined what happened today at the Sequoya restaurant. I fear that if I do not write this down immediately, I will later doubt my own memory and perhaps even my sanity. But before I record what happened today, I need to tell the story from the very beginning.

This story goes back twenty-five years in the 1980s when I was still a young journalist working some freelance assignments for a variety of Egyptian magazines. I had an assignment to prepare a piece on Siwa oasis.

Now Siwa of course has always been a place of mystery in Egyptian history. It lies some 300 kms west of the Nile delta smack in the middle of the Egyptian western desert, part of the great Sahara Desert. It is recorded that the oracle at the great temple of Amon at Siwa rivaled the oracle at Delphi.

Alexander the Great visited Siwa and consulted the oracle there. What he was told was never revealed, but History confirms that it was not good news. In fact, Alexander died in Mesopotamia under suspicious circumstances a couple of years later while returning from his campaign in India.

Another famous visitor to Siwa was queen Cleopatra VII, the one who was in love with Mark Antony. It is recorded that she visited Siwa and bathed in a spring there. Myth has it that this was a fountain of youth, and that is how she maintained her beauty and youth. The people of Siwa refer to this fountain as 'Cleopatra's Bath'. The location of the fountain was never determined. it was said that its location was a secret known only to the priests of Amon. But Cleopatra's trip to Siwa was of course documented and confirmed.

It is against the backdrop of this colorful history that I was preparing for my trip. I was to be accompanied by a young photographer. There is no direct road from the Nile delta. To get to Siwa one has to drive north to the Mediterranean coast and then west towards Libya. At the city of Marsa Matrouh one would then drive south deep into the desert for around 350 kms. The total length of the trip would is accordingly around 850 kms.

I was busy preparing for the trip when I got an unexpected call from my grandmother. She was a great lady, and apparently in her youth in the 1930s was a famous beauty at the court of King Farouk. She started the call as always by calling me by the nickname she had given me when I was a little boy 'Hello *ya afrit*'. An *afrit* is a sort of demon

(I must have been quite a naughty boy). I was quite surprised when she asked me if she could come along with me to Siwa.

Now you must appreciate that she was pushing 90 at the time. True she was still mentally alert and physically surprisingly energetic for 90 years old, taking long daily walks, but the prospect of taking her along to Siwa far from any proper medical emergency treatment, was daunting. I started to argue against this as not being a very good idea, but it soon became clear that her mind was set on this trip, and she would be terribly disappointed if I refused.

Who was I to refuse my 90 year old granny a wish that may be very well the last favour she asks of me. I accepted of course. Within a few days we were off leaving early in the morning, and after a long drive and one night spent at Matrouh we finally arrived at Siwa around noon the following day. We checked in at the only hotel in town. The photographer and I followed our pre-planned schedule with a visit that very afternoon to the temple of Amon that lay outside the town at the western edge of the oasis, a drive of about 15 minutes. My grandmother came along.

There was very little left of the temple, a few broken columns and boulders here and there and the whole site was covered with grass and trees, and surrounded with a dense expanse of palm trees. When we arrived at the temple it was totally deserted but for a solitary figure sitting on one of the fallen boulders. It was a man wearing a white robe. It was not a traditional *galabiya* that is worn by the majority of Egyptians outside the cities. It was different made of linen and covered with hieroglyphic characters.

In his right hand the man held what seemed to be a wooden staff. He was completely bald headed with a dark complexion. He stood up as we approached and bent low offering a strange salutation to my grandmother 'may the blessings of Horus be upon you oh daughter of Amon-Ra'. I immediately concluded that he was a local guide all dressed up in his showy costume and ready to offer us a tour of the site. I told him that we were fine on our own and needed no guide. I had prepared well for the trip and was not willing to listen to a load of drivel prepared by some ignorant local for tourists.

My grandmother, however, said that she would be happy to take a walk along with him and hear what he had to say. I saw no harm in this as it allowed me and the photographer to carry on with our work while my grandmother was kept entertained. The photographer and I started going around the site, he took photographs and I made detailed notes of some of the inscriptions on the stones and the general layout of the Temple structure.

Time just flew by, and before long we realized that it was nearing sunset. We had finished our work and were ready to return to the hotel. While the photographer started packing his tripod and equipment, I went looking for my grandmother. There was no sign anywhere of her or the guide. I became somewhat alarmed, and the photographer and I started calling out loudly for them. There was no answer, they had vanished.

Darkness falls quickly in the desert and before long it was pitch dark all around us. We drove back to the town and filed a police report at the police station. The locals all denied any knowledge of any bald-headed guide fitting the man's description. Apparently no such person existed in Siwa.

All sorts of horrible thoughts sprung to my mind. My grandmother had no jewelry or money with her when we left her, so that excluded robbery. What if that strange man was some maniacal psychopath? I shuddered as I imagined the worst. I spent a terrible night driving around Siwa looking for any trace of my grandmother. I stayed for a whole week in Siwa helping with the search, and only returned to Cairo when it was clear that there were no clues and no hope of unraveling the mystery of my grandmother's disappearance.

The authorities eventually filed the incident as a crime of abduction perpetrated by a person or persons unknown. My family never forgave me, and I never forgave myself for leaving my grandmother with a stranger. The years passed, as they are wont to do, fast and furious, taking me from one job to another, from one country to another. I spent some years abroad, and only returned to Cairo two years ago.

That brings me to what happened today at Sequoya restaurant in Zamalek. I was invited to lunch there by the editor in chief of one of the important Cairo dailies to discuss some articles I was preparing for them. Sitting at a large table next to us amid a group of people was a very beautiful young woman. She was in her twenties with a pale complexion and dark black hair cut at shoulder length. She was extremely attractive. I had a very strong feeling that I had seen her somewhere before. I could not help sneaking peeks at her every few minutes. At one point she became aware of my attentions and looked me straight in the eyes. For a moment what seemed like a flicker of recognition appeared on her face, and then she smiled radiantly at me.

I was amazed and enthralled. I was racking my brains to try and remember where I had seen her before. It was one of these memories that you know you have and will recall eventually, but the more you try to remember, the more it eludes you, and then much later when you are no longer trying it pops up from the depth of your mind. As the party she was with was leaving she passed close to our table and spoke to me. 'You are Mr. Tawfik the famous journalist?'

I stood up for some reason feeling like an awkward teenager in front of this woman who was half my age. 'I am not sure about the famous part, but yes I am a journalist.' She smiled and whispered 'you have made a success of your life *ya afrit...*' she winked at me, then turned around and left...leaving me standing dazed and speechless.

The voice was quite familiar, particularly the way she said '*ya afrit*'. It could not be! My mind refused to register what deep inside I knew was true. The memory that had eluded me now came unexpectedly back to me. I took hasty leave from my host claiming that I had forgotten an urgent errand and rushed back home.

I went straight to the closet where I kept an old suitcase full of old family photographs. Before long I had a photograph in my hand. It was in black and white and taken in the 1930s. It looked like it was taken at some formal dinner function, and there was my grandmother in an evening dress coming down some stairs. She had her hair cut exactly as she did at the restaurant and was smiling the same radiant smile.

I now know where she went that evening in Siwa many years ago with the priest of Amon. She went to take a bath. I wonder how many times she's bathed there over the centuries, and how she managed that trick with the poisonous asp.

If I ever see her again, I am sure I will ask her, and she may tell me, she is my grandmother after all.

The Temple

T was a young theoretical physicist just completing his Ph.D. in the nature of the space/time continuum at one of the top universities in the United States. He was invited by his parents to join them in a winter trip to Egypt where they would enjoy the sunshine and visit several temples of the ancient Egyptian civilization. T really needed a break, so he accepted. To his surprise he found the temples and information about ancient Egypt fascinating.

At one point they arrived at the town of Abydos some 100 kilometers North of Luxor. There they visited the great temple of Seti I, a pharaoh of the 19th Dynasty (built circa 1300 BC). The tour guide took them through the Temple explaining the different scenes depicted on its walls in colours that have survived for more than three millennia. Not far from the entrance they came across a group of hieroglyphs carved close to the ceiling. The guide explained that these were the famous enigmatic helicopter, submarine and jet plane engravings that have baffled Egyptologists. T looked closely, and yes, indeed, there was a very clear carved depiction of a helicopter, a submarine, and a jet plane.

At first, T could not believe what he was seeing. Then he was truly puzzled. As a scientist he could not believe what he was seeing. As the guide explained, the theory whereby Egyptologists ignored this vexing mystery was quite simple. In their view this was an error, several hieroglyphs carved together by mistake that coincidently made these shapes. T could not bring himself to accept this facile explanation. The probability of accumulated errors that would produce such clear pictures unprecedented in Egyptian hieroglyphs before or after the construction of this temple, was in the order of one in a several millions category.

T was mesmerized by the pictures, and totally baffled. After he returned to the States and recommenced his work on his thesis, he found that he was unable to concentrate. The mystery of the Temple pictures became an obsession. He had to find an explanation. After days of agonizing over this, he reached a conclusion. In his mind there was only one logical explanation. It was an explanation that he, as a theoretical physicist could accept. Time travel was the answer.

The more he thought about it, the more T became more and more convinced. Time travellers must have gone back to the time of Seti I and carved these pictures. Why a helicopter, a submarine and a jet plane were not clear. But it may have been a message to people living in an age where there were indeed helicopters, submarines, and jet planes. T analyzed the issue further. If the time travellers had carved futuristic machines, they would not have been understood by people in T's time. So, T became convinced that the message was indeed directed at people within his contemporary time.

T then directed his research to time travel. He understood immediately that the message hinted at three dimensions within which the three depicted machines could move freely. The problem was always 'time' that fourth quasi dimension knitted within the fabric of space itself. T decided to revisit the Temple and to look for further clues. To his parents' surprise he announced that he will revisit Egypt for a lengthy break from his studies. T went back to Egypt and spent a number of weeks at Abydos, visiting the Temple daily.

To the locals, he was just another *'khawaga'* (western foreigner) obsessed with the spiritual beauty of Abydos, the location that ancient Egyptians believed to be the place where all life commenced as a mound of land emerged from the primordial waters. Finally, T found his clues carved on the same ceiling not far from the three pictures. Translated from the hieroglyphic script they provided mathematical equations that solved the problem of the 4th dimension.

Using the equations that he found at the Temple, T returned to the US and worked very hard on developing a prototype for a machine that would pierce the fabric of space/time itself. He eventually succeeded but only in a backward direction. He found that he could send items back in time, but not forward.

The day came when T felt confident that he could try his machine on himself. He was careful to avoid time paradoxes, so he sent himself back 24 hours but in a different city. There he waited for 24 hours then returned home, thus avoiding meeting himself and disrupting the timeline.

He was now ready to go back to Egypt in the 14th century BCE to meet the mysterious time travellers who carved the pictures. He knew it was a one-way trip, there was no coming back. But he was hopeful that the time travellers will be able to help him in overcoming the obstacle of travelling forward in time. He prepared as much as he could. He studied ancient Egyptian history and language. He prepared a suitable wardrobe of linen clothes and medical supplies including anti-biotics and other emergency essentials. He prepared a reasonable quantity of solid gold and silver as currency. He took courses in sculpture and discovered that he had a real talent as a sculptor.

Finally, the date he had planned for arrived and he jumped back in time. He succeeded and found himself in ancient Waset (Thebes). His white skin and appearance did not raise any suspicions. Egypt had been for many centuries the 'melting pot' of the ancient world. Immigrants from Greece, the Levant, Nubia, Libya and other regions were welcome to live and work there, provided of course that they respected the local traditions and were loyal to the King (Pharaoh).

T as an accomplished sculptor was eventually hired as one of the supervising artists in the project to build the great temple of Seti I at Abydos. This is exactly what T had planned for, to get attached to the project in its very early stages, and then to keep his eyes open for the time travellers. The work was fascinating, and T became really immersed in the fine art of engraving all the wonderful figures of the Gods onto the stone walls. He was very good at his work and eventually was promoted to chief artist on the project.

The project took many years, at one point Seti I died, and his son Ramses II (Ramses the Great) ordered that the work on the Temple be continued (although he did add many references to himself and his 'glory' on the walls). T was very careful to observe all work on the ceiling where the pictures and the mathematical clues were carved. After eight years the Temple was near completion and still there was no sign of any time travellers.

T was becoming more and more anxious. Where were they? When the date of the grand opening was announced and all of Kemt (Egypt) was ready to celebrate, it finally dawned on T. There were no time travellers, he was the only time traveller around. T knew that once the Temple was opened and the priests took over, there would be no chance to make any changes.

Using his authority as Chief artist he ordered some last-minute engravings to be executed on the ceiling. His subordinates did not question his orders. This was Egypt and authority was revered, practically sacred and divine. The great and talented MeriAmon's ('beloved of Amon' in ancient Egyptian, the name adopted by T for himself) orders were carried out, although the artists were truly baffled by the weird drawings they were ordered to engrave. One drawing looked like a giant grasshopper, another like an inflated eel and the third was totally alien in shape. They also added other various hieroglyphs on the ceiling as directed by MeriAmon. The added hieroglyphs were all gibberish to them except for the very last one which they understood very well.

The Pharaoh was delighted with the work in the Temple and T was very generously rewarded. He spent the rest of his life travelling around Kemt working on the divine Pharaoh's various and stupendous building projects, including the great temple at Abu Simbel on the borders of Kush (Nubia). He never married and did not beget any children.

A curious event happened after T's sudden disappearance in the 21st century. Egyptologist noted, apparently for the first time (although they could not understand how this could have been missed before) a hieroglyphic inscription at the end of the ceiling inside the great Temple of Seti I that contained the famous enigmatic drawings.

In hieroglyphic script this read 'MeriAmon sends his love to his dad and mom'.

Thus Danced Zarathustra

Sunrise

Thustra was moving quickly now carrying the young one under one arm and his spear in his other hand. He darted right and left to avoid the occasional rocky outcrop. The hyenas were not far behind. This pack had been following the People now for several days and have picked up and killed a number of stragglers during the night. Their screams had filled the sky and the hearts of the young ones with terror.

From beyond the memory of the oldest of the elders, the Life Speakers who recounted Life around the fires, the People have been moving. How many have they left behind to hyenas and other beasts only the spirits could know. Recently the spirits have been speaking to Thustra when he lay at night traveling to the other world. Their faces sometimes appeared in a heavy fog, and they seemed to smile at him.

Now as he ran only one thought hammered in his mind... Get the young one to safety! This little girl he carried had wandered outside the camp that they had set with the fires surrounding the huddled groups of People. Thustra as one of the spear carriers had not hesitated. He went out in the dark night, as have others, to search for her and fetch her before the hyenas found her.

Now he saw the faint glow of the campfires in the distance and he felt some hope in his heart. They may still make it back. From somewhere deep inside him he gathered some additional strength and increased his speed. But then he stumbled on a jutting rock and fell. As he fell, he lifted the girl as high as he could to shield her from the rocky ground.

The hyenas closed in; their eyes gleaming in the darkness. He stood up and pushed the little one behind him. He went into his fighting stance. He stabbed the first beast that attacked them in its belly and began to pull back his spear, but two others had closed in. One beast bit Thustra in his left leg tearing at the flesh and muscles. Thustra could feel the blood flowing.

Suddenly there was a cry and several spear carriers from the camp appeared. They carried sacred fire in their hands. The hyenas growled but moved back. Slowly the group with Thustra limping but still carrying the young one walked slowly back to the camp. This would be a story worthy to be told by the Life Speakers around the campfires.

Next day the People reached a great river. A river greater than the greatest river ever spoken of around the campfires. There were no words to describe it. Thustra and the rest of the people just stood on the shore and looked in wonder at the far shore. It was just a small tip of land surrounded by water so vast that to both sides there was no end to it. There was only that distant tip with mountains behind it.

The People could not recall mountains. These were only mentioned by the Life Speakers as things that lay in the memories of the spirits. But they knew that mountains had caves, and caves meant safe shelters and good fire pits. The water of this mighty river was salty and not at all sweet like the waters of the countless rivers crossed by the People in their long journey.

That night as the People sat around the fire, the spirits spoke through the Life Speakers. The dancers began dancing and the singers began singing. Moving slowly and singing in a low voice to start, and then faster and faster, louder and louder, everybody eventually joining in the steady rhythmic dance and chant. The spirits promised good game beyond the great river and the far mountains at the other shore. They promised Life without hyenas. The People danced and chanted their voices rising into the night to mingle with the lights of the spirits that shone and twinkled high above them in the clear sky.

Thustra could feel the blood still flowing from his leg wound. An old one had bandaged it for him putting some of the magical red leaves on it. The pain was very strong, but he did not cry out or moan. He knew that just before dawn they will cross the great river, and he should not show weakness. Despite the pain he danced and danced, twirling round and round, letting the People's chant wash over him. Finally, exhausted he fell asleep, only to be woken by the Elders to get ready for the crossing.

The great light of the world's birth had started seeping slowly from under the lid on top of the sky, red like the sacred fire. The young ones were placed on wooden logs to be pushed along. The old and sick would also cross. Everyone crossed, such was the People's way. Those who could not swim sank below the waves to join the spirits in the other world, to be remembered around the campfires.

The pain in Thustra's leg was now nearly unbearable. He limped to the shore and went into the water. Before him he pushed a log with some spears and skins on top. He swam with slow but powerful strokes. All around him the people swam. The little ones sitting astride logs and being pushed along by the strongest of swimmers. The little ones were very precious, loved by all. Through them the voice of the spirits and the Life Speakers will continue.

This was truly a great river and even after many heart beats the far shore was not getting closer. Thustra had lost much blood and was getting weaker. He looked up and could now see the Great Ball of Fire begin to rise in the sky. He could now make out the far shore and the far mountains. He did not feel fear. If he sank beneath the waves someone else will take care of the log with the spears and skins, and he, Thustra, will finally join the spirits. There were many questions he wanted to ask them. Why did the People have to move all the time? Why were they hunted by the beasts? And many other questions that were in his mind.

Finally, he saw that he was nearly there, not very far from the shore. He felt exhilaration, he might still live to see the mountains and what lay behind them. He could see that some of the People had already crossed and were lying exhausted on the beach. He tried to swim faster. Then he looked around him and saw that there were others still struggling in the water. The little girl he had carried the night before had fallen off her log and a woman who was pushing that log was having difficulty in getting the little one back on top. They were thrashing and struggling in the waves.

Thustra pushed his own log towards the shore and swam back to the woman and the little one. It was not easy going back as the waves were now higher. He finally reached them and helped the woman put the little one back on top of the log. The woman then pushed the log in front of her as she swam through the waves towards the shore.

Thustra started to swim along beside her, but suddenly he felt the muscles of his right leg cramp up. He was very tired and his hands could hardly move. He kept his head above the water with difficulty, and the waves were becoming even higher.

Thustra looked and could see that the woman and the little one were now very close to the shore. He was happy that they will cross and will not sink into the other world. He felt weaker and weaker and was now swallowing some water. It was salty not sweet like the water of the other rivers that the People had crossed, and he coughed it out.

With a last spurt of energy, Thustra turned and looked back to the land the People have left behind. He then looked at the far mountains beyond the shore. He squinted as the Great Ball of fire rising above the mountains, and he could see some green patches on top of the mountains. He even thought he saw a herd of gazelles. He looked again, there was nothing there. He smiled because he knew that the spirits have spoken to him again and that now he understood what they were saying.

Thustra sank slowly beneath the waves.

Thus Danced Zarathustra

Song of the Night Wanderer

The boat rocked violently from side to side. The waves were getting higher. Zara looked around her. She could see fear in the eyes of the huddled People. The young ones were placed in the middle of the crowded boat. The People as instructed by the captain and his mate, had not carried any belongings with them, just the clothes on their backs. Some children had small toys that they clung to. But the parents had nothing. The sound of the engine was high and deafening, and spray was coming over the side soaking many of the People.

They were told the trip to the tip of Italy would take two days and nights, and that when they arrived, they would be met and taken care of. Each family on the boat had paid the captain of the boat all their life savings to buy their place on that crowded deck. It was clear to Zara that the captain had been greedy. After two days and one night there was no sign of Italy, and the small boat was quite low in the water with its overcrowded human cargo and all the water that had seeped in. This was their second night on board, and Zara felt that the boat would not last till the morning.

The People had no choice, in the land they had left behind human beasts roamed, and death was always present or just around the corner. Death with its ugly obscenity and terrible finality. Zara was with her uncle and her uncle's family on board the boat. Her parents had perished when their village was bombed many weeks ago. She remembered the black clouds of smoke that hung over the streets for days blocking the sun and filling the air with the acrid smell of burnt homes and dreams.

The bombardment lasted for a few days. The bombs came regularly one after another. One bomb every few minutes. It was as if the soldiers who were surrounding the village had only one gun. They could make out the smoke from the gun in the distance a second or two before each shell landed. The rebels hiding in the village refused to surrender. When the last rebel fell under sniper fire, one of the village elders walked out in the direction of the gun's smoke waving a white flag.

The bombardment stopped. When the old man had covered about half the distance, the sound of a single shot echoed, and the old man fell to his knees and then slumped forward.

When her home was hit Zara was out fetching water. The crumpled bodies of her parents were hardly recognizable. Dead, they looked small and helpless. Zara did not cry right away. Death in all its horrifying forms had become quite common in her small village. She had seen children crushed under the rubble. Children burnt and carried in the arms of wailing mothers.

Zara did cry for her parents but this was much later after the soldiers were done with her. When at last the soldiers had left the village, and she lay naked and bruised, she did cry. She cried for days and days and all the tears that were inside her flowed down and down and watered the barren and broken parts of her soul. She never cried again.

The only thing that kept her alive after that was her dancing. She had always loved to dance and was the best dancer at school. At home she used to twirl around and around, and her parents would laugh along with her, sharing in her happiness. That evening after her tears had dried out, she had gone into the quiet night amid the ruins of her village and had started dancing and twirling around and around. From then on, she danced every night from sunset to dawn. The people who remained at the village called her the night wanderer. They felt sorry for her. Some would cry and hug her; others would look away in shame.

She suddenly stood up and even amid the crowd of people in that little crammed boat, she started to twirl around and around, with her hands up in the air. It was strange and magical, but someone started clapping the beat to her movements, and then one by one the rest of the People joined in. They clapped and she twirled and moved her hands. She looked up at the clear sky and when there was no spray, she could see the stars twinkling like little candles.

The boat capsized before dawn. Zara had fallen asleep, and she woke with a start when she heard someone scream. There were loud noises, and she felt the cold-water rush across her lap as the middle sea claimed their little boat.

Zara stood up and looked around, it was still dark, but there was a hint of light on the horizon ushering in the new day. She looked for her uncle and his family. She could not see them. Now the children were screaming, and the men were shouting, as if with their angry bellowing they could bring order and justice to the world.

All of a sudden, Zara found herself submerged in water. She kicked and kicked and made it to the surface. She found a large wooden plank, part of the boat, and clung desperately to it. She saw on her right her little cousin, he was only five years old. His head was bobbing up and own in the water. There was no sign of her uncle or his wife. She reached out and grabbed the little boy by his hand and pulled him to her. He clutched her neck, and she could barely stay afloat by holding on to the large plank.

Zara finally managed to make the little boy grab the plank and pushed him so that he sprawled half way across the plank. He was sobbing silently. She tried to comfort him by singing one of the songs that her mother used to sing to her. She sang in a deep voice 'hush little one and go to sleep... have beautiful dreams...tomorrow I will cook for you a tasty dish... tomorrow you will play and play... hush little one and go to sleep.' Eventually the sobbing stopped.

Time passed,Zara felt like she was in horrible nightmare that would never end. The sun rose high, and she had to shut her eyes from its glare. There was no one around, just herself, the child who was now asleep sprawled on the large plank, and the vast blue sea.

Sometime later, it could have been minutes or hours, Zara saw a boat far away. She wanted to shout and scream for help, but she had no energy left. She could not even raise her hand. When she looked again the boat appeared bigger, it was getting closer and closer. She could not think straight, but it seemed that they would survive after all. She wanted to smile but could not even do that. As the boat loomed beside them, she could see that it was a small fishing boat. On its side were the words 'SPERANZA' clearly the name of the boat.

A young man leaned over and took hold of the child's arm and pulled him onto the fishing boat. He then leaned over and pulled Zara over the side and onto the small deck. There were only two persons on board. The young man who had pulled her up and an old man. On the deck there were fishing nets piled in the center. The child lay by the boat's side sleeping on his back.

The young man brought Zara a blanket and some water. She looked at the child and could see that they had covered him with a blanket, even his head. Good she thought, now he could be warm at last. They spoke to her in a foreign tongue, she knew it was Italian. She did not understand anything they said. She tried to thank them. She muttered 'thank you' in her own tongue bringing her palm up to her heart. They spoke urgently with each other. They seemed to have reached a decision. The old man turned the wheel and revved up the engine. The young man started to stow things on deck.

The young man then brought Zara some bread and cheese. She ate and found out that she was famished, she swallowed down the food hardly chewing. Never had she tasted anything better. Suddenly she felt guilty and looked at the sleeping child. She gestured to the young man pointing to the child and to her mouth, indicating that the child also needed food. The young man looked at her. There were some tears in his eyes. He shook his head slowly and looked down at his feet.

At first, she did not understand. She went and lifted the blanket that covered the little one. He lay unmoving on his back. His eyes were closed. His lips were blue. She did not cry. She was unable to cry anymore; all her tears were gone. She slumped down and held the dead child's head in her lap and started singing to him again 'hush little one and go to sleep... have beautiful dreams...tomorrow I will cook for you a tasty dish... tomorrow you will play and play... hush little one and go to sleep.'...

That night when the SPERANZA docked in the small fishing village, the people who saw her coming in were surprised to see a figure of a girl on the small deck twirling around and around with her hand pointing up to the twinkling stars...

About the Author

Khaled El Shalakany is an engineer and lawyer. He holds degrees in engineering, law, management and Egyptology. He has a number of published books, including a number of collections of short stories and a novel in the Egyptian vernacular. He lives in the town of El Gouna by the Red Sea, north of Hurghada, Egypt.

Printed in Great Britain
by Amazon

31137082R00129